Pride Publishing books by Thom Collins

Jagged Shores

SAFE HARBOUR

THOM COLLINS

Safe Harbour
ISBN # 978-1-83943-752-6
©Copyright Thom Collins 2021
Cover Art by Kelly Martin ©Copyright November 2021
Interior text design by Claire Siemaszkiewicz
Pride Publishing

Published in 2021 by Pride Publishing, United Kingdom.

SAFE HARBOUR

Dedication

In memory of Mark Kendrew, an exceptional
friend.

Chapter One

"Will you be staying long in town?" the shop assistant asked as he ran items through the till.

"Two weeks," Matt Ramsey replied.

"Really?" The assistant, a pleasant-looking man in his fifties, didn't look up from what he was doing. "It's a small place to spend such a long amount of time. Won't you get bored?"

"I doubt it. I want to use Nyemouth as a base to explore the local area—country walks, coastal trails, that kind of thing."

"Oh, then you'll find plenty to keep you busy. There are some stunning locations nearby, both up and down the coast."

Matt smiled. He'd already done extensive research into this area of Northumberland. He'd visited here a couple of times before, just for the day, and it was a place he'd always wanted to discover further. With two weeks ahead of him and no other commitments, there would never be a better time.

He had finished work at five p.m. promptly and got straight into his car. Despite the Friday evening traffic, he'd made good time on the journey from York to Nyemouth, arriving at the holiday home just before seven-thirty. The old man who lived next door, a friendly guy called Jacob, had greeted him at the door with the keys and given him a quick rundown on the property and what he could find in town. Matt had left home without picking up supplies, and Jacob directed him to the small shop near the marina, less than ten minutes from the house, where he could get all he would need to see him through the next few days. Matt had thanked him and hurried down to the store.

He intended to get a takeaway for dinner tonight, but picked up bread, eggs, bacon, milk and tea bags for breakfast. He also bought three bottles of red wine, a bottle of dark rum and two litres of Diet Coke. It was his intention to eat out as much as possible while he was there, but he wanted to have some alcohol in for the times he came home late, so he could unwind in the comfort of the beautiful house that looked down on the marina and the mouth of the river.

"Have you lived here long?" he asked the cashier as he paid for his shopping.

"All my life," the man said, sounding proud. "I know I knock the place for being small and there's not a lot to do here out of season, but I do love it. I can't imagine living anywhere else."

Matt nodded. "Even in the winter, I imagine it's still a lovely place to be."

The man gave a good-natured laugh. "Come back in February when there's a seventy-mile-per-hour gale coming in from the North Sea and see if you feel the same."

"If the next fortnight goes well, I might just do that."

"Well, if you do, I'll be here." He handed over the two bags of groceries. "Enjoy your stay. Hopefully I'll see you around."

Matt thanked him and left the shop.

That evening, it was difficult to imagine the brutal winter conditions the shopkeeper had spoken of. It was coming up to nine o'clock and the clear sky was deepening into shades of lapis and blueberry, marred by just a few wisps of cloud, high in the atmosphere. The perfect sky was mirrored on the still water of the harbour. The fishing fleet was home for the night, the boats lying motionless in their moorings.

There were a lot of people milling around the marina, couples and families enjoying the mild July weather. The bars and restaurants along the waterfront had set tables outside and looked to be doing a good trade. Matt had heard great things about The Lobster Pot, a bar-come-restaurant in the heart of the bay, and intended to treat himself to at least one good meal there during his stay — maybe one night next week when it wasn't so busy.

He walked across the harbour, passing by the lifeboat station, towards the footpath back up to the house on South Bank Terrace.

Nyemouth's lifeboat had made worldwide news the past summer when it was involved in the frantic rescue of the actor Arnie Walker and his young son. The publicity afterwards had brought hordes of tourists to the small seaside town. When Matt had been searching for a place in Northumberland to stay for his summer holiday, he'd almost discounted Nyemouth, remembering the scenes of chaos he'd seen on the news less than a year before. He wanted somewhere peaceful as a base for his hiking trips, and the interest Arnie's rescue had created for the town made it far from ideal.

Matt had done some extra research and, while it was true that Nyemouth was now on the map as a major tourist attraction, the initial ghoulish interest people had taken in it had settled down, although he'd read that Arnie Walker was now a permanent resident here with a home on the north bank of the river. When Matt had discovered a house on the south side was available for the dates he required, those niggling concerns had disappeared.

Now he was here, breathing in the fresh sea air, and he knew he'd made the right choice.

At thirty-nine, Matt had no qualms about going on holiday by himself. He was a free man, able to do what he wanted and pursue his own interests without having to compromise for someone else. Some of his friends and colleagues had tried to talk him out of it and persuade him to join them for his summer break. Matt had no interest in their Spanish villas or their all-inclusive trips to the Caribbean. He'd always wanted to explore Northumberland, and now, divorced and one year short of his fortieth birthday, he intended to do exactly what he pleased.

Those same colleagues were always trying to fix him up with their gay friends. It was four years since he'd split with Clinton, and people seemed determined to pair him off with someone else.

It was all well-meant, but Matt didn't need it. This was his time to do his own thing, and he intended to enjoy it.

He followed the path upwards, through the cobbled backstreets of the old town. Living in a city, albeit a modest one like York, gave him a greater appreciation of small towns and villages, especially those on the coast. The pace was much calmer here, more peaceful. He knew he was looking through the rose-tinted eyes of a tourist, but tonight he was happy in the belief that life was simpler in a place like this.

A middle-aged couple walking a small terrier smiled at him and nodded as they passed.

"Hey," he said in return.

After a busy day at court, he looked forward to a quiet night in the holiday home. He would pour a glass of wine, order some food and unpack his stuff while waiting for it to arrive. He was too tired to explore the town this evening. There would be plenty of time for that tomorrow. He intended to get acquainted with Nyemouth this weekend, checking out the shops, pubs and cafés, before exploring the wider area next week.

Matt was a keen walker and hiker. Though the path from the marina to the house was steep, he managed it with the two bags of shopping without getting even mildly out of breath. The path levelled out as he reached South Bank Terrace and the last stretch was straight. The views from up here were second-to-none, taking in the entire valley and the river mouth. Maybe he'd be able to enjoy it with a glass of wine in the front garden before darkness cut in.

There were two men on the path that ran in front of the garden wall. He heard their raised voices as he approached.

"I've told you a million times before that the answer is no," one of the men said. He was dressed in running shorts and a T-shirt—younger and slimmer than the other man. *Pretty hot*, Matt noticed the guy with long, muscular legs and dark brown hair that swept back from his face in luxurious waves.

"You're being unreasonable," the second man said. His voice sounded tight, like he was speaking through gritted teeth. He was stocky and thickset, with closely cropped grey hair and a narrow face. He wore grey suit trousers and a white shirt, the sleeves rolled up and the neck open.

"You're the one who followed me up here," the younger man said, sounding like he was close to losing it.

"What was I supposed to do? You won't answer your damned phone. You don't respond to my voicemails."

"Don't you get it, Vince? I blocked your number. I've told you before—I don't know how many times—but I've had enough."

A lover's tiff, Matt guessed, though they seemed an unlikely couple. The young guy could do so much better for himself. Not that looks were everything, but he was way out of the older man's league. Matt gave them a wide berth as he passed, but came close enough to see just how attractive the young man was. He had large, expressive eyes, a long, straight nose and a wide mouth. He looked wholesomely handsome in his running gear, giving off cute Clark Kent vibes.

The other man, he realised, was not as old as he'd first seemed, maybe early-to-mid-thirties. His prematurely grey hair and sharp features created a false impression. Even still, the two men did not look well matched.

"Just come with me," the older man, Vince, snarled. "Listen to what I have to say."

"Vince, I've heard everything before. There's nothing you can say now that will make any difference."

"How do you know if you won't give me a fucking chance?"

Matt opened the gate and carried his shopping to the front door. He would not get involved. As a lawyer, he spent his entire working life dealing with the relationship problems of other people. These were two grown men. They could sort out their own issues. He put the key in the door.

"Get off me," the young man snapped.

Matt glanced back to see him pull his arm out of Vince's grip, and the man immediately lunged for him again. The young man dodged the grip.

"Stop being such a prick," Vince said, his voice much louder now.

Matt groaned. This had the potential to get out of hand. He'd witnessed this kind of behaviour so many times—not just through work and handling messy divorce proceedings, but at home. Throughout his childhood, his father had been a pig, quick to anger and keen to use his fists. Matt didn't want to get involved, but he couldn't ignore this either.

"Is everything okay, fellas?" he asked, turning to face them.

Vince snapped his head around in his direction. "Piss off and mind your own fucking business. Prick."

Matt ignored him and directed his gaze at the younger guy.

The man forced a smile. "It's fine. Really."

Matt nodded, unconvinced, but reluctant to involve himself any further in what was clearly a domestic argument. He carried his bags inside and through to the kitchen. As he put his supplies into the cupboard and the fridge, he could still hear their raised voices.

Vince sounded like the worst type of man — the kind of inadequate dickhead who tried to compensate for his own shortcomings with bullying and aggression. Matt knew the type well, having grown up with one until the age of twelve, when his mother had finally thrown his father's sorry arse out. And he'd represented so many women and children during divorce and child protection cases who'd been caught up in relationships with controlling men.

Although he wanted to leave them to it, Matt's conscience wouldn't allow him to. He went into the living room and watched them through the window, hoping their argument would die down before it got any worse.

The young man had his hands up, warding Vince off to no effect as the little man puffed himself up and tried to get in his face.

"You stupid little prick," he heard Vince say. "You're worthless, you know that. *Nothing*. You were no one when I met you and you're no one again."

The skin of the young man's face and neck was flushed. "If that's how you feel, why don't you go? Go on, and leave me alone."

"I can't leave you alone," Vince said, changing tack. "You need me, Jake. You can't get along without me. You're useless on your own. You can't cope."

The young man, Jake, turned his back and tried to walk away. Vince grabbed his arm again and hauled him around, pulling him close, then wrapped his arms around him, taking him in a bear hug.

"Let go of me," Jake protested.

"Enough of this shit. We're going home." Vince tried to lift him up and carry him.

Jake struggled, twisting out of his grip. Vince raised his hand to strike him.

Matt had seen enough. He pulled his phone out of his pocket and turned on the video camera as he headed for the door. He was filming when he stepped outside, training it on the two men. They might not like it, but he was determined to have a clear record of what happened next in case he had to call the police to deal with them.

As Matt walked down the path, Vince hauled back and struck Jake, his fist connecting with the side of his face, sending the young man sprawling to the ground.

"What the hell?" Jake complained, scrabbling backwards in the dirt, shuffling on his butt to escape his attacker.

"Stop pissing about and get the fuck home," Vince jeered. "I've had enough of this fucking around. Do what I tell you to for once."

Matt's own anger mounted. Now that things had turned violent, he couldn't let it continue. "Pack it in," he shouted, coming to the end of the garden path.

Vince twisted in his direction. Matt saw the uncontrolled emotions flicker across his face — surprise, confusion, anger, then the aggression was back. He bared his teeth like a feral dog. "I've told you once already. Piss off and mind your own business."

"I was prepared to do just that," Matt said, keeping his voice calm and even, like a headmaster addressing a petulant teenager. "But when you throw your fists about, I can't let that go. And, yes, I got that punch you just threw on camera, in case you're wondering. It's something I'm sure the police will be interested to see."

Vince's focus flickered between Matt and Jake. The bastard was no longer so sure of himself.

"This is a private matter. Nothing to do with you or the cops." He puffed out his chest as he spoke, trying to assert his manhood.

"Again," Matt said, amazed by his own composure, "that was the case until you started punching in the street. Now, it's very much a matter for the police. Why don't I call them and see what they think about it?"

"You fucking busybody... You should stop twitching your curtains and getting involved in things that have nothing to do with you."

Matt kept the camera trained on him. "You're not very bright, are you, Vince? For the third time, *you* made it my business. Now, are you going to take yourself off down that hill, or do I have to call the police to do it?"

Vince strutted towards the garden gate. "Why don't you try to make me? Show me if you're man enough to take me on." He clenched his fists.

Matt wouldn't fight him, but there was a good chance Vince would take a swing at him, regardless. "We have different ideas of what makes a man," he said. "Violence won't get you anything other than jail time, Vince. Even if Jake there doesn't want to press charges against you, my testimony and video evidence will be enough to charge you and get you in front of the local magistrates on Monday. Is that the way you want this to go? To spend the weekend in a police cell? Or would you rather leave before you make it any worse?"

Stalemate. They glowered at each other across the fence. Bigger and more menacing men than Vince had tried to intimidate Matt, and he had not backed down. He wasn't about to cave under the glare of this prize arsehole.

Vince's face twisted in an ugly expression before he spat at the ground. He stepped away, turning his back on Matt. "Are you coming?" he demanded of Jake, who had risen to his feet and stood brushing the dust off his shorts. Matt noticed a smear of blood on the younger man's face.

Jake shook his head. "Just go — and leave me alone. I don't want to see you again."

Vince loitered, his fists still clenched, his arms trembling.

There's so much anger simmering under his lid that he looks like he's about to explode.

"I think the message is clear," Matt said. "Why don't you do everyone a favour and leave?"

"Fuck you," he said at last, his voice low and contemptuous. And as a parting shot to Matt, "Cunt."

He strutted down the road, his shoulders back, knees wide, trying to look like a big man.

Matt, realising he'd been holding his breath, exhaled.

This was not the quiet evening he'd intended for the first night of his holiday.

Chapter Two

Matt opened the gate and approached Jake, who stood watching as Vince walked away.

"Are you all right?" he asked.

Jake's skin was rosy, and his chest rose and fell dramatically. His hands trembled. *Shock*, Matt surmised. Jake turned to look at him. His eyes were wide, the pupils huge. "Yes," he said, out of breath, "I'm… I'm fine."

"You're bleeding."

"What?"

Matt pointed at his cheek. "Where he clocked you."

"Oh." He put his fingers to his face and looked at the blood on the tips.

"Why don't you come inside for a few minutes? I'll get you an Elastoplast for that."

"No, I couldn't. Sorry… We've caused you enough trouble already."

"Hey," he said softly, "don't apologise. I couldn't ignore what was happening. Come on in. You're shaking, too. Take a seat until you get your breath back.

Give your buddy time to get away. I wouldn't want you bumping into him at the bottom of the road."

Jake exhaled, and the tension left his neck and shoulders. "If it's no trouble, I could come in for a few minutes — just until things calm down."

"Are you hurting anywhere else?" he asked, leading Jake to the front door and inside. "From when you fell."

"Only my pride," he said. "If that counts."

Matt smiled. "Nothing wrong with your sense of humour." He led Jake to the kitchen at the rear of the ground floor and sat him at the table. Matt folded a piece of kitchen roll into a small square and gave it to Jake. "Press this tight against the cut. There's a first-aid kit in my suitcase. I won't be a minute."

"No need," Jake said, pressing the paper towel against his cheek. "This should be enough to stop the bleeding. It's just a scratch. You've done more than enough already. Thanks a lot."

Being so close to him, Matt realised what a great-looking guy Jake was, with those beautiful eyes and unblemished skin. His T-shirt was well-fitted, showing the fine shape of his chest and shoulders beneath. His bare arms were muscular, gently suntanned and covered in light-brown hair. Despite his serious expression, there were very few lines on his face. Matt guessed his age to be around twenty-five.

"Do you want me to call the police?" he asked. "I got most of what happened on camera — certainly, the assault part. With me as a witness and the video evidence, they'll have enough to charge him. It'll get him out of your hair for the weekend, at least."

Jake shook his head. "I don't want to involve the police. It will only make things worse."

"That guy assaulted you."

"I'll live. It's just a scratch. If we phone the police, it will only make Vince more upset."

Matt didn't push it. He'd seen this so many times before when victims of violence didn't want to pursue a case for fear of inflaming the situation. "So, who is that guy? Your boyfriend?"

Jake exhaled dramatically. "If only. That would make things so much easier. No, Vince is my husband — soon-to-be ex-husband. At least I hope so. That's what tonight was all about. My solicitor wrote to him about the divorce and he got the letter this morning."

"And Vince refuses to co-operate, right?"

"Spot on. He says he won't give me a divorce. So, I'm having to fight him all the way."

Matt nodded sympathetically. It was another familiar story, one he encountered often in his career. "How long has it been? Since you separated?"

"It's coming up to a year. I moved in with my stepsister late last summer. I've been trying to get him to consent to the divorce ever since, but he won't have it."

"How long were you married?"

"Four years. It's a long story. I won't bore you with the details, but I should never have married him."

"You must have been very young."

"I was. Twenty. My mother and stepfather died suddenly in a car accident. Vince was so supportive afterwards. He stayed right at my side all the way through. Whatever I needed, he took care of it. It was only much later that I realised he'd taken advantage of me when I was at my lowest. I was in a daze for months after the crash and didn't know what I was doing. I really thought he was the man for me, except he didn't show me the kind of man he really was. Not then. That didn't come until much later."

"Like the man I saw tonight?"

Jake shrugged. "Kind of, though he's never really been violent before. He used to lose his temper a lot, but it was more verbal aggression than anything physical. Vince likes to be in control of everything, and he didn't like it when I stopped relying on him so much."

Matt said nothing. He'd heard variations on this story almost every week from the partners of inadequate, narrow-minded men. There were a lot more guys like Vince around than the average person would suspect.

Jake removed the paper towel from his face. "I think it has stopped. Just a scratch. Thanks again." When he smiled, two deep dimples cut into his cheeks. They made him look so much younger and boyishly handsome.

Matt looked at his watch. "It's only been a few minutes. I don't think you should go out there just yet. He might still be hanging around at the end of the road."

"Okay. Thank you. You're probably right. It kills Vince when he doesn't get the last word, so this—your intervention—will have pissed him off."

"I can drive you home if you like. If you think he'll be a problem, it could be safer."

Jake looked directly at him with those wide, blue eyes. "That's a lovely offer, but I'll be fine. You've done enough already. Really, I'm grateful for the chance you've given me to step away from the argument. And I don't live far. I was on my way home when he ambushed me on the path out front."

"How about a drink while you wait?" Matt offered. "I only arrived this evening, so I have little to choose from, but there's wine or rum, if you like either of those." He pulled the bottles out of his shopping bags. "I was about to open the red, anyway."

Jake looked like he was about to refuse, then thought again. "Okay, if you don't mind. A glass of wine might take the edge off my nerves. Thank you."

"You don't have to keep thanking me," Matt said, searching the cupboards until he found two glasses. The bottle had a screw top, so he didn't need to keep looking for a corkscrew.

"Sorry. My mother was a stickler for good manners. That has never left me." He sighed and stretched. As he raised his arms to ease out his shoulders, Matt glimpsed soft brown hair in his armpits. The sight was surprisingly erotic.

Matt put the glasses on the table and sat facing him. "I suppose I should introduce myself. I'm Matt."

Jake flashed a wide, genuine smile, showing nice white teeth. His eyes sparkled. It looked to Matt like he had recovered from the worst of his experience.

"Jake," he said. "But you know that already after the piss-poor performance out front."

They shook hands. Matt caught a waft of his aftershave or deodorant, something fresh and light. It suited him. "Pleased to meet you."

Jake sipped the wine. "Are you staying here long? In Nyemouth, I mean?"

"A couple of weeks. I want to do some walking and sightseeing."

"Cool." Jake cast his eyes slowly around the kitchen. "Lovely house. I know the guy who owns this place, but it's the first time I've been in here myself. He only started renting the place this summer."

"Really?"

"Yeah, Dominic. He's a great guy. I'm a volunteer down at the lifeboat station. Dominic is on the crew. He did this place up himself. Apparently, it was pretty run-down when he bought it. The house is really old. From what I understand, it's one of the oldest in town. This whole terrace is."

"It's perfect now." Matt had done little besides take a quick look around when he'd arrived, but the house surpassed his expectations. It was often the case when renting a summer cottage that the reality failed to live up to the glossy perfection presented on the letting website. That was not the case here. If anything, it was more charming and atmospheric than the ads. The modernisation of the property had been done with respect for its age and history.

"It is," Jake said. He flicked his focus around the kitchen and through the double glass door to the private patio out back, before returning to Matt. They held eye contact for a couple of seconds before Jake broke it, gazing into the depths of the wine. "The guy who lives next door, Jacob, is the treasurer at the lifeboat station too."

Matt laughed softly, surprised at how quickly he had warmed to Jake. He was always cautious with strangers, taking a long time to let down his guard, but talking to this young man in this new place, he felt very much at ease. "Jacob gave me the keys when I arrived. Is this one of those towns where everybody knows everything about each other?"

Jake sat back, seeming to give the question some thought before answering. "No more than anywhere else, I suppose. I grew up in Newcastle, where we didn't know many of our neighbours, and I saw none of my friends outside of school, so it took a while to adjust to a small town like this when we moved here. It was an enormous culture shock at first. But I think the locals are friendly rather than nosy. I run a café in town with my stepsister Lizzie, so I probably know more people than most. And the fundraising we do for the lifeboat involves spending a lot of time in the community. So maybe I'm the nosy one. I seem to know everyone." He laughed and took another sip of wine. "This is nice. I don't drink a lot of wine, but I really like it."

Matt swirled the red around the glass and tasted. "Mm-m. I picked it up at the shop in the marina."

"Oh, yeah. You'll have gone past our café, in that case. We're in the harbour, halfway between the shop and The Lobster Pot. It's called The Seagull. Why don't you come in sometime and let me make up for your help tonight? It's all homemade stuff. I cook the breakfasts and prepare all the meat and fish dishes for lunch. Lizzie does all the baking. Her cakes and scones are the best in town."

Matt looked up in surprise. He hadn't expected this to be anything more than it was — helping out a stranger in trouble. Now Jake had offered a line for them to stay in touch. Under normal circumstances, he would have jumped at the chance to get to know the guy better. Jake was a little too young for him, but there was no denying how attractive he was. But Matt had just witnessed how turbulent Jake's life was. Matt dealt with jealous husbands most days of the week and he'd come on holiday to get away from all that. Besides, his own personal life had just settled down. He didn't need the complications of Jake and Vince right now.

He's offering you a coffee, he remembered, *not the key to his heart.*

"Well, I'm here for two weeks," he said. "I'll check it out sometime."

"Please do. I'm not kidding when I say we're the best in town," Jake added cheekily. "The Lobster Pot is nice if you want something fancy, but when it comes to good, honest grub, we can't be beaten."

"All right," Matt relented with a grin. "You're on. I want to check out Nyemouth this weekend before I explore farther afield. I'll pay you and Lizzie a visit when I'm out wandering."

"Excellent." Jake knocked off the rest of the wine. "I should go and leave you in peace. If you only arrived an hour or so ago, you can't even have unpacked."

"I haven't. But there's no need for you to rush off. What if Vince is still hanging around out there?"

"I doubt he is," Jake said, getting to his feet. "If he waited at all, he'll have figured I've gone into Jacob's next door. Vince is scared of him. Jacob is in his seventies, but he doesn't take any nonsense. He must be out for the evening, because if he'd heard us arguing, Vince would be in the back of a police van by now. The old man has never liked him and would have called the cops in a second—either that or call for some of the lifeboat crew to come up here and give Vince a taste of his own medicine."

"I like the sound of Jacob," Matt said, also standing. Now he was torn. He wanted to be left alone to get on with the quiet evening he'd had planned, but now that Jake was leaving, he didn't want him to go. He wanted to discover more about this intriguing young man.

Which means it's time for him to leave, he told himself. This kind of attraction, however innocent, was no good for either of them. The best thing for him to do was to stamp on it now.

He walked Jake to the door. "Are you sure you don't want me to run you home?" he offered. "I've barely touched my wine. I'll be all right to drive."

"Quite sure," Jake said. "I can't thank you enough for what you've done already. I'm not sure I'd have been as willing to break up an argument between two guys, but I'm glad that you did."

He shrugged, keeping it light. "Hey, what did I say before? There's no need to keep saying thank you."

"I want to, all the same. Make sure you stop by the café so I can give you lunch."

He nodded. "Okay, I promise I will."

"We're open every day, though I don't work Mondays."

"Noted."

"Okay, then. Nice to meet you, Matt. Hopefully, I'll see you again soon."

Jake closed the garden gate behind him and walked off down the road. The sky was deep blue now, almost navy, and Matt wondered whether he should insist on walking him down the hill in the near-dark. He was being ridiculous. Jake was a strapping lad. Tall and muscular, he could look after himself.

As he stood on the doorstep and watched him depart, Matt's spirit gave an unexpected lurch, as Jake turned and waved at him before disappearing down the path.

What a lovely guy, he thought. If their circumstances were different, there could have been a potential for romance there.

Except romance was the last thing he wanted right now.

Chapter Three

Jake Wrangler rose at five-thirty most mornings. By six-thirty he was in the kitchen of The Seagull Café preparing for the early breakfasts when they opened at seven. It was always busy, even more so at this time of year, with visitors looking to get a good meal in them before starting out on their fishing expeditions and sightseeing trips. Most days the work was routine, and Jake went through it on autopilot—opening up, starting the ovens and boilers, preparing the joints of meat for the lunchtime service. He could do it all with his eyes closed.

Which was just as well this morning, because his mind was elsewhere — mainly on the events of the night before. He'd gotten very little sleep as he'd turned it all over in his mind again and again.

When Vince had jumped out at him during his run, it had been no great surprise. Jake ran along the coastal paths several nights a week, and Vince knew the routes he took. He'd been expecting a visit from Vince at some point that week, knowing that his solicitor had sent a letter to Vince regarding the divorce proceedings. Vince remained adamant that he would not consent, that their marriage was not irreparably broken and if Jake would just come home, they could make it work again.

It had been no surprise either when Vince's plea for a reconciliation had turned to anger and ultimately violence. Jake had lived with him long enough to know the routine. After all these years, Vince was nothing if not predictable.

Jake hadn't expected an intervention from a good-looking stranger. He had expected no intervention at all. For five years, he'd had to deal with Vince's anger and temper alone. Matt's appearance had seemed to take Vince by surprise. Like a lot of bullies, he was not used to being challenged. It had been fascinating to see the change in his temperament, how his hard-faced expression had transformed. In an instant, he was not so sure of himself. Jake had only ever seen that uncertain side of Vince once before, on the day he'd packed his cases and left.

Jake had also been surprised at the relief he'd felt when Matt had invited him in. Matt had made a good call, because Vince would certainly have been waiting for him at the bottom of the hill. He would not have gone far right away.

Jake sighed and turned the bacon on the grill, positioning half-tomatoes around the slices. His insides were in knots as he continued to relive the events in his head.

And Matt. He couldn't stop thinking about Matt, and not just for the obvious reason — his great looks.

Matt could be one of the most handsome men he'd ever seen in Nyemouth. He was in the same league as Dominic Melton, his crewmate on the lifeboat, and

Arnie Walker, Dominic's handsome fiancé, a famous actor. Matt had the same dreamy movie-star features — lush dark hair, all wavy and thick, going just a bit grey at the sides, and intense, pale blue eyes. Jake had felt as though they'd pierced him when Matt looked at him. He had the most gorgeous facial features — chiselled cheekbones and a firm jaw, with a sexy cleft in his chin. He had a good growth of stubble, also peppered with grey. Jake wondered how old he was — older than Vince, but not by much. He could be in his late thirties, forty at most.

He was a hundred percent better looking than Vince, that was certain, and completely out of Jake's league.

Though that would not be an issue. Vince had done enough to put Jake off men for a long time. Matt was a hottie, but Jake had no intention of doing anything other than looking.

He continued with his work. Sandra, the waitress who worked the early shift, came in just before seven and opened the front doors. From then on, the breakfast orders started, and Jake didn't have time to think about Matt, Vince or any of his personal problems. It was just as well. Work had kept him sane for the whole of this last year, ever since he'd walked out of the house.

Vince had wanted him to give up the café — to forgo his independence and stay at home, keeping house for his husband. It was a ludicrous idea, one Jake had initially laughed at, but Vince had been deadly serious. He not only wanted Jake to give up the business, but to step down from his position on the lifeboat crew.

Vince had pretended his request was motivated by concern, that he didn't want Jake working long hours in the café and risking his life at sea, but Jake saw it for what it was — an attempt by an increasingly desperate man to cut him off from his family and friends and control him. At twenty-six, Jake was not the lost, bereaved boy Vince had married. He didn't need a replacement father, and he loved what he did.

Jake had no intention of being subservient to any man ever again. When the divorce was finally settled, he would only be interested in a relationship of equals.

Lizzie came in just before nine. Running the café with his stepsister was the perfect combination. Jake came in early and finished around three most days. Lizzie arrived later and kept the place open until after five, then together they doubled up over the busy midday period.

"Morning," she called cheerfully, going straight to the sink to scrub her hands. At thirty, she was a few years older than he was. Black and beautiful, she had a lively personality and a cool head for business.

"Hey," he called, "I missed you last night. Did you stay with Kelly?"

"Yes. We had a quiet one, bingeing a show on Netflix. It got so late I decided to stay over."

As well as running The Seagull, Jake and Lizzie shared a house. Lizzie was no fan of Vince and had invited Jake to stay with her the second he'd said he was leaving him.

Lizzie dried her hands and put on a clean, white chef's tunic.

As Jake set up a plate of toast, poached eggs and smashed avocado, he caught her watching him from the corner of his eye.

"What happened to your face?" she asked. "You've got a scratch."

There was no point in lying to her. Lizzie could smell bullshit at a thousand paces. He told her about the incident with Vince on South Bank Terrace. "Don't lose your temper," he warned. "There was no actual harm done." He put the breakfast plate on the heated pass-through and hit the bell for the waitress.

"And if it hadn't been for this tourist guy stepping in? Then what? He'd have given you a black eye, gotten in a few punches. That smarmy bastard. I'll kill him when I get my hands on him."

"What did I just say? Calm down. Nothing happened. I can handle Vince. I'm not afraid of him."

"You should be. He cut your face, Jake."

"It's a scratch, that's all. It didn't bleed for more than a few seconds."

"He's done it before, hasn't he? Knocked you around?"

"Leave it."

"I bloody knew it. I said as much to Kelly. I told her that shit used to hit you. I've always thought as much."

"Lizzie, forget about it. It's over. I left him, remember? He can't do anything to me now."

"It looks like he had a pretty good go at it last night. Did you report him to the police?"

He sighed. "No, I didn't want to make things worse. You know what he's like. If the police turned up, he would have gone ballistic. Besides, they've got better things to do with their time. I'm a grown man, and I can handle it."

She pursed her lips. Lizzie meant well, but she was overprotective at times. Since both of their parents had been killed in a crash, Lizzie saw herself as his guardian. He loved her for it, adored her, but he was a grown man now. When he made mistakes, he had to fix them himself, not rely on his big sister.

"You should get a restraining order against him," she pressed on, undeterred.

"I'd rather just get the divorce. That's all I can focus on right now. I can't move on until it's over."

Thankfully, they got a sudden flurry of big orders, which diverted Lizzie's attention. For the next forty minutes they got their heads down over the cookers and grills. Jake didn't want to think about Vince anymore. His brain was overloaded. The solicitor handling the divorce had told him it could drag on for years if Vince resisted it. Jake couldn't bear to think about that. Surely Vince would accept that he was never coming back and sign the papers.

More than anything, Jake wished Vince would meet someone else. He used to goad Jake during their heated arguments, saying how easy it would be for him to find a replacement, a younger, hotter man. If it were so easy, Jake wished he would hurry up and do it.

When the breakfast rush was over, Jake set about the lunch prep. The joints of turkey, beef and pork he'd put in the oven first thing were almost done. He put huge pans of potatoes and carrots on to boil and more potatoes in the oven to roast. Even at the height of summer, the café still did a huge trade in roast dinners. With The Lobster Pot and a fish-and-chips takeaway on the same street, The Seagull offered something different that people seemed to appreciate. It also sustained them through winter. When the tourists had all gone home, their hot dinners were a big draw for the locals.

Around eleven-forty-five, just before the lunch trade started, Sandra came in from the front and tapped Jake on the shoulder. "Vince is outside," she whispered. "He wants to see you."

Jake was grateful for her discretion. Lizzie was making dough for the afternoon tea service and would likely have charged through to confront him with a rolling pin if she'd heard.

"Just popping out for a breath of fresh air," he called across the kitchen to Lizzie. "Won't be long."

She smiled, giving him a thumbs-up gesture.

Jake took off his apron and hurried through to the front of the café. He was glad to see Vince waiting outside. He didn't want an argument in front of the customers.

It was a bright day with a crisp breeze blowing along the marina.

Vince, dressed in a charcoal suit, must have come there straight from work. Though it was Saturday, he often went into the office to keep things running smoothly.

As Jake stepped out, he jerked his thumb towards the waterfront, wanting to get Vince away from the café. If Lizzie knew he was there, it would end one of two ways. She'd either call the police or attack Vince herself.

"Have you signed the papers?" Jake asked.

"Of course I haven't," Vince said, his eyes twinkling. "I love you. I will *not* sign away what we have together."

Jake suppressed a groan. "Then what are you doing here?"

Vince spread his hands. "I came to apologise. Things got a little out of hand last night."

Jake pointed at the scratch on his face. "You mean this? Is this what getting out of hand looks like?"

"What can I say?" He smiled. "I love you so much that my emotions get the better of me at times. It's only because I have so much passion for you that I get so worked up. C'mon… You know the way I feel about you."

Vince didn't love him, Jake knew that now. It had taken four years of marriage for him to realise it. Vince wanted to control him, wanted to own him, but that wasn't love. "Is that all you came to say? I've got work to do."

"Don't be unreasonable. I came to tell you I'm sorry. The least you can do is accept my apology." He used the tone of voice Jake had gotten used to and come to loathe. The condescending adult speaking to a petulant and unreasonable child. "I even want to buy you dinner…tonight. How about we go for drinks then a meal at The Lobster Pot? All on me. I'll pick you up around six."

Unbelievable. "No."

"What do you mean, no?" Vince gave a smirk. "I'm trying to be nice, and you throw it in my face."

"Like your fist last night? You threw *that* in my face."

"Darling, come on. I've said that was an accident. How much more do I have to do?"

"You can sign the divorce papers. That would make me happy."

Vince ignored the remark and pressed on, undeterred. "I tried to make it up to you last night. What happened? I waited for you down here, away from that nosy prick with the camera, but you never showed up."

And there it is. The real reason for this visit. Vince would have been eaten up with suspicion, wondering where he had been.

"I'm going back to work. Bye."

"Hang on. I'm asking a question. Where were you? Did you go in to see old man Jacob or what? You couldn't have come down any other way."

Jake kept a lid on his simmering anger. He didn't want his customers to witness a scene. Vince had made more than enough of those lately. "Stay away, Vince. I mean it. I only want to see you again if you've got the signed papers in your hand."

He heard Vince's mocking laugher behind him as he headed back to the café.

"You'll be waiting a long time for that, sweetie. A fucking long time."

Jake kept his chin up and plastered a smile on his face as he went back inside. Several of their customers had heard Vince's last outburst and turned to see what was happening out front. His insides twisted as he headed to the kitchen. He'd spent the last year trying to get rid of Vince. It didn't look like the ordeal would be over any time soon.

Chapter Four

The house on South Bank Terrace was so tranquil that Matt abandoned his plans to explore the town on Saturday morning and spent the time getting acquainted with his new surroundings. He'd stayed in bed until almost nine—a rarity for someone used to getting up at six-thirty most days—and opened the curtains on the incredible view of the town and marina below. It would have been worth staying there for that sight alone.

It looked like around half the fishing fleet had gone out for the morning, while the tourist boats that would run visitors out on trips along the coast were gearing up for business. Glancing seaward, he took in the blue sky, but the water looked choppy with white caps on most of the waves. Matt didn't care much for the idea of heading out to sea in those conditions. He would think twice, even if the sea was flat calm, but he supposed most others would find them perfect.

After a shower, he'd put on a pair of cream-coloured shorts and a navy-and-white striped T-shirt and headed down to the kitchen. Despite the nasty incident with Jake and Vince that had sullied the first night of his holiday, he had slept well and awoken with a massive appetite. He brewed a pot of tea, then grilled two slices of bacon and fried an egg, assembling them in a breakfast sandwich, which he ate outside on the rear patio.

He was in no hurry to move afterwards. Protected from the breeze, the patio was so relaxing. He eased back into the oversized cushions and abandoned all his plans for the morning. Nyemouth was a small place. He'd have plenty of time to explore it this afternoon.

His thoughts drifted to Jake, wondering whether he'd got home okay. Despite his determination to keep out of it, he couldn't help feeling some sympathy for the younger man. Matt knew exactly how messy relationships and divorce could be, and not just from a professional perspective. He'd had first-hand experience of the emotional shit-fest. Even now, four years after his own divorce had been finalised, Matt couldn't put it all behind him.

At least Clinton had never been violent. That was one thing Matt's ex had over that prick Vince.

Clinton had many faults. Matt had thought he'd known them all when they'd got married, taking him for better or for worse. *Yeah, right.* What he'd known about Clinton at the start had just been the tip of the iceberg. Clinton was a man with little self-control. Matt had thought he could handle that. It was just a minor fault with an otherwise sexy, charismatic and funny man. He'd discovered while they were on honeymoon that Clinton's lack of control ran to forty thousand pounds in gambling debt.

Matt had been pragmatic. He'd increased their mortgage and paid off the debt. It had been naïve of him to think that would be the end. Clinton was a compulsive spender, a man who always had to have the best of everything — clothes, cars, watches…and other men. It shouldn't have come as the shock that it had when he'd discovered Clinton's second phone — the one with the Grindr app installed, the one he used to meet all those other guys.

After the discovery of the phone, all the other lies had unravelled. An additional sixty grand of gambling debt, a failed attempt to re-mortgage the house behind Matt's back, a secret boyfriend as well as his random Grindr hook-ups. Those underhand betrayals had been the final straw.

The fact that they both worked for the same legal firm had complicated their divorce further. They practised at different branches and only ever saw each other at the monthly partners meeting. Despite all the lies and deceit, Matt was prepared to maintain a professional distance and move forward.

After they'd sold their house in Leeds, he'd bought his own apartment in York, close to work, and begun his new life.

Clinton had not been so successful. His compulsive behaviour continued unchecked — drugs, gambling and sex. He had no control over his appetites. Only recently, four years after the divorce, Clinton had been fired from the firm. The senior partners had tried to keep a lid on it. The official line was that they'd dismissed him for gross misconduct. They wouldn't tell Matt any more than that. He'd got the real story from the junior staff who worked at Clinton's branch. His behaviour had become more erratic — missing appointments, failing to turn up at court. The bosses had been on the verge of sacking him anyway. When he'd been caught snorting cocaine in the bathroom at work, it had been the final nail in his coffin. Clinton was out.

Matt had felt terrible for him. He still did. Clinton might have brought on his own demise, but Matt couldn't reject the feelings he used to have for him. He was now working for a tiny law firm in a little town in Yorkshire, lucky to get any job at all after what he'd done. He'd hit Matt up for cash a couple of times in the last four months — not enormous amounts, just enough to see him through until payday, he'd said.

Matt couldn't refuse.

He had the greatest sympathy for Jake now. The circumstances of his marriage to Vince would be different from Matt and Clinton's, but divorces were all pretty similar. They hurt — even more so if Vince refused to consent and dragged it out. It could take Jake years to get free of him. Matt hoped he had an excellent lawyer. He would need one.

Another thing Matt understood about men like Vince… Once he accepted that a divorce was inevitable, he would fight hard to hold on to everything he could, including things he wasn't entitled to. And partners like Jake, worn down after years of battle, often gave in and surrendered everything just to be free.

Matt guessed it was a sure bet that Vince would go after Jake's business, just to hurt him.

He didn't envy Jake the pain the next few years would hold.

Not my problem, he reminded himself. He found Jake incredibly attractive, but he would *not* get involved.

When the teapot was empty, Matt carried the dishes back into the kitchen and washed up. It was almost midday. *Wow.* He really had kicked back this morning and lost track of the time, but he felt no guilt about that. He'd been working hard in the last few months — even more so in the weeks leading up to this break, trying to get ahead with his cases and making sure the files were in top shape before taking time off. Matt was no stranger to long hours. It was uncommon for him to get home before seven-thirty most evenings, and he always brought files back to work on at the weekend. He intended to forget all about work for the next two weeks. No emails, no messages, nothing.

He walked through to the front of the house, wondering what to do with his afternoon. He wanted to check out the town and stop into some of the pubs later, maybe even have some dinner down there rather than another takeaway.

Matt opened the front door and stepped out into the bright sunlight. While the rear patio was sheltered on all sides, the forward-facing garden offered an expansive view. The sun was high, and a fresh wind came in off the sea. In that instant, he decided what to do next. He'd put on his walking shoes and a hoodie and take a wander along the clifftops behind the house. He'd fill his lungs with that salty air before heading into town for a few beers and a bite to eat later.

Jacob, the old man next door, was pulling weeds out of the borders of his garden. He straightened up at the sight of Matt. "Hey there. Settling in okay?" he asked.

Matt walked to the waist-high fence that divided the properties. "I definitely am. That's the best night's sleep I've had in…well, I don't know how long."

Jacob smiled, adjusting his cap against the glare of the sun. "It's the sea air," he said. "There's nothing better for ensuring a good night. Even at my age, when I don't sleep as long as I used to, I still feel well rested afterwards. I won't want to be anywhere else than here."

Matt smiled. "Have you lived here long?"

"Most of my life. I had a few years away in my teens and twenties when I served in the army, but Nyemouth has always been home. My family has been here for generations. I moved into this house when I got married, and I've always said the only way they'll get me out of here is in a box." His blue eyes twinkled as he said it.

"I can understand why. It's lovely."

"It's a shame you had such a poor start to your holiday last night. I hope it didn't give you a bad impression of the town. I can assure you that Vince Ashfield does not represent the people of Nyemouth. Vince is bad news. Even as a kid, he was a little shit. Nothing has changed, except perhaps his temper, which is worse these days than ever before."

"Oh, you saw all that?"

Jacob nodded. "I was dozing in front of the TV when they woke me up. By the time I got to my feet and came to see what the commotion was all about, you'd seen him on his way. That was good of you. And taking young Jake in until Vince had gone? That was a smart call. I'd have come out and done the same if it looked like he was going to go after Vince."

"It seems like they have a lot going on."

"Jake's a good lad. He should never have taken up with an arsehole like Vince. Vince took advantage of him. Jake's parents weren't even cold in the ground before Vince got his hooks in. He made Jake rely on him. The boy didn't need him. He's smart and brave too. He'd have dealt with his grief in his own way and got on with things. Lizzie, his stepsister, she'd have looked after him. Vince made his move when Jake was at his most vulnerable."

"It sounds like you know Jake well."

"I suppose I do. He came here when he was around fourteen. That was when Jim Elba married his mother, Melanie. They were a lovely couple. Jake had been raised in the city his whole life, but he took to the water like he'd been born to it. He had an instant fascination with boats, which was just as well in a town like this. He started helping out around the lifeboat station straight away, getting involved in our fundraisers and keeping the place tidy. Then, as soon as he was old enough, he signed on for the training and joined the crew. He's been with us ever since."

Impressive. Going out in a boat on the open sea was terrifying to Matt, even on a calm day. That Jake would volunteer to go out in the worst conditions to rescue someone in trouble was astonishing.

"So, you're a member of the crew yourself?" he asked.

Jacob chuckled. "Not at my age. I was for a long time, though. Thirty-four years I was part of that team. I'm an old man now. I play my part behind the scenes. It takes a lot to run a station like ours in a busy town like Nyemouth. We're a charity and rely on public donations to keep the service running. Young guys like Jake are the lifeblood of the organisation."

"That's amazing."

"The station will be open for visitors this weekend. Take a look if you're passing by. There's a little public gallery and souvenir shop. Every penny counts."

"I will," he said. "Absolutely. I'm going down there soon."

Jacob adjusted his cap again. The heat of the sun had intensified in the time they'd been talking. "I don't suppose you will, but if you bump into Vince Ashfield again when you're looking around, don't let him give you any crap. He's all mouth, that one. If he sets up to you, call the police and report him. It's about time someone did."

"Don't worry," Matt assured him. "After last night, I have no intention of wasting another minute of my holiday on that guy."

Jacob gave a warm smile. "I'm glad to hear that. You've got your head screwed on right, unlike a lot of people. Well, I'd best get back to the plants and let you get on with your holiday in peace. You know you can knock on my door if you need anything. I'm always happy to help."

"I appreciate it. Thanks."

"And if you happen to enjoy a nice tot of whisky, I've always got a bottle of the good stuff on the go. Drop by one night and see for yourself."

Matt thanked him and went back inside to get his walking boots. Jacob seemed like a genuinely nice man. Except for Vince, everyone he had met so far in Nyemouth had been friendly and welcoming. Matt intended to keep to himself as much as possible these next two weeks, but it was good to know he had a friend next door if he got lonely. That wasn't something he'd ever been able to count on in all the other places he'd stayed.

He went upstairs and got his boots out of the wardrobe. He'd unpacked all of his stuff the previous night. He put them on and took his navy hoodie in case it was cool up on the point. As he grabbed his phone off the dresser, he realised he hadn't switched it on. He did that now and went back downstairs. As he retrieved his wallet and keys from the kitchen, the phone sounded its message alert.

He took a quick look at the screen. Five missed calls and two text messages. He tapped into the caller log and groaned.

The missed calls and messages were all from one person – Clinton.

Delete them. Don't read them.

Clinton knew he was on holiday. They'd last spoken three weeks before, and Matt had stupidly let it slip in their conversation. The no-doubt urgent messages had been timed to drop a shit-bomb on Matt's time away.

Against his better judgement, he opened the first text.

Hey. Sorry to bother you. Wouldn't ask if I wasn't desperate. Can you loan me a couple of grand? Please. XOXO.

Matt sighed and shoved the phone into his pocket. He wasn't even going to answer. Clinton already owed him a thousand from earlier in the year – money that Matt knew he would never see again. He would not throw good money after bad to help his ex settle another drug or gambling debt.

The days of him being a sucker were over.

Matt headed for the front door, determined to worry about no one but himself for the next two weeks.

Chapter Five

By Sunday, the North Sea breeze had dropped to almost nothing, and the sky was a clear blue. Nyemouth swarmed with tourists making the most of the brilliant day. The north shore beach was packed with holiday-makers as children and couples frolicked in the sea, enjoying conditions more accustomed with the Mediterranean than Northumberland. The town was just as busy, with bars and restaurants appreciating a great trade, their outdoor seating areas crammed to capacity.

Matt had spent a few hours exploring the quieter back streets. The temperatures were more bearable in the shade. He liked the sun, but not to the blistering degree it offered around midday. Like most seaside towns, there was a lot to discover away from the busy thoroughfare of the marina and beaches. He found a gallery of seafaring artwork and several antique shops where he lost the best part of two hours. He found an exquisite set of bronze and marble bookends that would look great in his apartment in York. The price was steep, and he was in no mood to haggle with the owner today, but he would keep an eye on them during his time there and see if he could talk the price down before the end of the fortnight.

There was an excellent second-hand bookshop where he whiled away another hour before picking up a mint first edition of *The Carpetbaggers* by Harold Robbins and an acceptable copy of *Jaws*, which he figured would make as good a summer holiday read as anything else he'd find. He remembered his mother devouring both books when he was a kid and had always wanted to read them, though she'd refused to let him, saying they were too grown-up.

Around three o'clock, he found himself back in the marina, looking at The Seagull Café.

He'd discovered it on his walkabout the previous afternoon, but something had kept him from going inside. Maybe it had been the text from Clinton, but Matt hadn't been in the mood for company or conversation yesterday. Today he was in a much better frame of mind and eager to check in with Jake again.

The young man had never been far from his thoughts. The events of Friday night still bothered him, and though he was determined not to get involved in young Jake's marital problems, it would settle his mind to know he was okay.

There were tables on the street outside, and it looked like The Seagull was a popular choice this Sunday afternoon. Matt's innards knotted as he stood there, unable to see inside because of the sun reflecting on the window.

It's too busy. Jake won't have time for an idle chat.

He wavered, unable to decide whether or not to go in, and was confused about his unease. Why should it bother him so much? Jake had told him to drop by.

He'd been walking for hours and hadn't eaten since that morning. He could do with a drink and some refreshment.

Before he had time to change his mind, Matt strode inside.

The interior was cool — air-conditioned — and after the glaring sun in the marina, it took a few moments for his eyes to adjust to the gloom. There were plenty of empty tables. It appeared everyone else wanted to eat in the direct heat of the sun.

As Matt's vision came into focus, he looked to the counter.

And there he was.

Jake.

Something inside Matt lurched at the sight of him.

Jake, busy ringing something into the till, didn't look up. "Take a seat," he said, cheerfully. "Someone will be over in a minute."

He came out from behind the counter with someone's bill and the change on a metal tray. He wore black trousers and a dark T-shirt with a navy apron tied around his tight waist. He looked gorgeous and kind of harassed. A lock of hair had fallen out of place and hung over his forehead, reinforcing one of the first impressions Matt had had of him — Clark Kent. There was a pink flush of exertion to his face and a light sheen to his skin. Matt had forgotten how strong his arms and biceps were, the suntanned muscles working perfectly with the dark colours of his uniform.

Jake was much sexier than he remembered — and his memories were hot.

"Oh, it's you," Jake said, looking up as he headed for the door. He stopped where he was. "Matt, so good to see you. Thanks for dropping by." His smile illuminated the entire room.

"Hey," Matt said, feeling shy and unsure of himself—more like a skittish teenager than a thirty-nine-year-old lawyer. "I just wanted to see how you were doing. I was passing, so thought I'd call in."

"I'm glad you did. Listen… I've almost finished my shift. Have a seat. Just let me take this change out and I'll be right with you." Jake carried the plate to one of the tables outside.

Matt exhaled in relief. He'd broken the ice. Why did that seem like such a big deal? *It isn't.* He'd only met Jake once before, for less than half an hour on Friday night. He had no expectations of him. This was a friendly catch-up, checking in with the stranger he'd helped out of a sticky situation. Nothing more.

Matt sat at a table facing the window, so he could watch the action in the harbour. He picked up the menu. The Seagull looked like they offered everything—breakfast, lunch, afternoon tea, snacks. There was also a large blackboard on the far wall, detailing the daily specials. Today's offers were local scampi with chips, peas and homemade tartare sauce, fresh crab salad or seafood stew. Matt glanced over his shoulder to the counter and saw a large selection of cakes, cookies and scones. The aroma inside the café was mouth-watering.

"So," Jake said, coming back inside, his smile at full wattage revealing those cute dimples, "how hungry are you?"

"Not very," Matt answered truthfully. He hadn't eaten since breakfast, but there were so many butterflies fluttering about his stomach he had no appetite. "I could do with something light. Maybe a sandwich."

"How do you feel about seafood? I know not everyone likes it, but we've got some beautiful white crab meat. It came fresh off the boats this morning. I cooked and picked them myself."

"I don't think I've ever tried it before."

"Okay, let me make you a crab sandwich. If you hate it, I'll get you something else. What about something to drink? Beer, wine, soda."

"What goes with crab?"

"I would go with a dry Chardonnay."

"Sounds great. I'll take your recommendation."

He watched Jake's face. The stubble seemed heavier today than on Friday, and he wondered if he'd let it grow in a little to hide the scabbed-over cut on his face from Vince's punch. If Matt hadn't been looking for it, he might not have noticed.

"I won't be long," Jake said, flashing another brilliant smile before disappearing out the back.

Matt's pulse raced. He realised how giddy he was. It was crazy. Jake had him tied up in knots. Was he really such a sucker for a pretty face? *No.* Matt knew it wasn't that. There was more to Jake than his great looks. He perceived a warm soul behind that beautiful exterior.

And it was obvious the attraction was mutual. The way Jake looked at him and the force of that smile spoke volumes about the way he also felt.

Nothing would happen. Matt wouldn't let it. They both had far too much going on. But what harm could there be in a little friendly flirting?

Jake returned a few minutes later and Matt was pleased to note that he'd brought two glasses of wine with him. He'd also removed his apron.

"The food won't be long," he said, setting down the glasses and sliding into the chair opposite. "How is your holiday so far? Are you enjoying it?"

"It's been even more relaxed than I intended." Matt told him about his slow exploration of the town, how he'd gone no farther than a mile along the clifftops when exploring. "I'll make more of an effort this coming week. I want to check out some of the Northumberland trail and discover the entire coast. That's the main reason I came here."

Jake nodded and sipped his wine. "I suppose those are all things we take for granted when we live in a place like this. We don't see half of what the tourists come here for. It's a shame."

"What do you do to relax?" Matt asked.

"I don't get a lot of free time. This place keeps me busy. I'm here at six-thirty most mornings. There are lifeboat meetings and crew training exercises on evenings and weekends, as well as any call-outs. And I've got a boat of my own, so I spend all of my spare time either working on her or sailing her."

"Wow. Your own boat. That's impressive."

"Don't go imagining a grand super-yacht or anything fancy. She's a small cruiser called *The Golden Lady*. I inherited her from my stepdad and have done my best to look after her ever since. Even small boats are expensive, so I do as much of the maintenance as I can myself. I've had to learn a lot over the last few years, but I know my way around an engine pretty well."

"That's amazing," Matt said. "I mean it. I get seasick on a ferry, so the thought of setting out on one of those boats in the marina is terrifying — never mind going out on a lifeboat in a storm."

"I love it. I love everything about boats. There's nothing better than sailing out of the harbour and getting my lungs full of that salty air, feeling the wind in my hair. Nothing compares to it." His eyes glistened as he spoke. Matt was sure he could detect something of the ocean in their complex blue depths.

He wondered how such an outgoing and plucky young man could have gotten embroiled in a toxic relationship with a guy like Vince. Jacob must have been right in his estimation, and Vince had preyed on him at a vulnerable time. It was hard to imagine the man sitting across from him now being so susceptible. At least he'd been strong enough to walk away.

The food arrived. Two identical plates of sandwiches on wholemeal bread, with salad and what looked to Matt like fresh coleslaw.

"I'm starving," Jake explained, as he took one of the plates. "I had a coffee around eleven, just before the lunchtime rush, and haven't stopped since."

"Are you still working now?"

"No. Lizzie does the last few hours in the kitchen and closes up. She's not really a morning person, so I take the early shift. I finish between three and four most afternoons, depending on how busy we are. It's often earlier than that in the winter, but at the height of the summer, we work as long as it takes."

Matt picked up the sandwich and took a bite. He'd never tasted crab before, and it was delicious — sweet and succulent. "This is not how I imagined it. I always thought crab would be…well, fishy."

Jake chuckled. "Not the white meat. It's lovely. The brown flesh can be an acquired taste. We don't serve that to the customers much, not unless they ask for it. A little in our crab cakes, but that's about it. The local cats are fans of the stuff, though. But the white is delicious. What about lobster? Are you a fan of that?"

"I've only tried it once, but yes, I liked it."

"Then check out The Lobster Pot while you're here. You won't get anything better. If I want a special treat, it's always at the top of my list. We're spoiled for choice with fresh seafood here in Nyemouth."

"Do you fish yourself?" Matt asked. "Seeing as how you have a boat."

Jake chewed and swallowed before answering. "No. Fishing involves too much patience and sitting around. I have to keep busy. I like to take the boat up and down the coast, but I never stay still long enough to put a line out. You should come out with me sometime."

"Oh, no," Matt said. "I really don't have good sea legs. I much prefer to look at the water from the shore than be out on it. Thanks for the offer, though."

"If you change your mind, you only have to ask. I promise to take it easy on you." There was more than a hint of suggestion in his final line. Jake pulled a small order book out of his pocket, along with a pen. He wrote hastily. "Here's my number. If you change your mind, let me know. You'll see things along the coast from the sea you can never see on land."

Thrilled, Matt pocketed the number and finished his sandwich. The taste of the crab went perfectly with the white wine Jake had chosen. When they'd finished eating, he asked, "Have you had any more trouble from Vince since Friday night?"

"No. He came by yesterday, supposedly to apologise, but in reality he asked me to get back with him. Nothing has changed. He still refuses the divorce, so it looks like I might have to wait it out, however many years it takes — which is a pain. I could really do with my half of the money in the house to get started with my own place. I'm living with Lizzie at the moment, which is great, but I promised her it would only be short-term. I might have to start looking for a place to rent until I can afford the deposit on a mortgage. Either way, it's a lot better than living with Vince, I can assure you of that."

"You could have reported him on Friday. That was domestic assault. If you got it on record, it would go in your favour with the divorce."

"That's what Lizzie said too. But I don't want to involve the police in a private matter. I'd rather we sorted it out between us."

"I've kept the video I took. If you change your mind, the evidence is always there."

"Thanks. But I hope it won't come to that."

A loud electronic alarm interrupted them. Matt started as Jake leapt to his feet and pulled a small pager from his pocket.

"I've got to go," Jake said. "Lifeboat call. It was great chatting to you. Please come by again." Then he raised his voice and shouted in the direction of the kitchen. "Lizzie, I've got a shout. I'm off."

Jake raced for the front door and disappeared.

Matt got to his feet and saw the back of Jake's head as he hurried through the crowds in the direction of the lifeboat station.

"That thing nearly always gives me a heart attack," a voice beside him said.

Matt turned to find that an attractive black woman dressed in chef's overalls had come through from the back of the café.

"You should hear it in the middle of the night. Even through two closed doors, it frightens the life out of me," she said.

"What happened?"

"The coastguard must have raised the alarm. They need the lifeboat to go out. When the pager goes like that, Jake runs. It looks like a calm day out at sea, but those are often the worst. A lot of these day-visitors don't realise the strength of the currents around here. They can be playing in the shallows one minute, and the next they're half a mile out to sea and unable to make their own way back. As beautiful as our beaches are, they're dangerous places to be if you don't pay attention."

* * * *

From across the street, concealed by the crowds of people gathering in the harbour, Vince Ashfield watched as Jake bolted out of The Seagull and ran across the waterfront. He knew exactly where he was going. He'd seen Jake shoot off like this dozens of times before. The lifeboat had an emergency call.

Vince had believed throughout their marriage that Jake thought more of that damn boat than he did of anything else. No matter what time of day the pager went off, Jake would drop everything and run.

Vince had asked — no, demanded — that Jake give it up. Nothing should have been more important than their relationship. It was the one subject on which Jake refused to budge. Nothing Vince said or did made any difference. There was one time when Vince had taken him to The Lobster Pot as a treat. Jake was always banging on about how much he loved the food there. They had only just ordered and poured their first drink, when the pager sounded. Without a word of apology, Jake had scrambled from his seat and shot off to the station, leaving Vince to finish two whole lobsters on his own.

He'd made sure the little bastard lived to regret that decision all right, but it had made no difference in the long run. When the next emergency had arisen, Jake was there.

For the first time, Vince was glad to see his husband racing to the station. The pager looked like it had gone off at just the right time to break up that cosy little scene he was having with the interfering bastard from Friday night.

Vince didn't believe they'd met each other by coincidence just two days later.

He'd spotted the smarmy fucker walking through the town earlier and had followed him at a distance, curious to know where he was going, certain he would end up at The Seagull. Vince's intuitions were never wrong, and the man had gone straight there. Then a few minutes later, there they were, Jake and the stranger making cow-eyes at each other across the sandwiches.

They planned to get together this afternoon. No doubt about it.

Vince had been suspicious of what Jake got up to on Friday night after he'd left him alone up there. Jake had let him believe he'd called in on old man Jacob. *Bullshit.* He'd been with this smooth bastard. He was sure of it now.

Neither of them had wasted any time — slipping into the house for a good time the second his back was turned.

That was why Vince had to keep Jake on a short leash. He was young, still controlled by his hormones and his dick. When a good-looking cunt like this one gave him the eye, he was bound to drop his pants and give it up.

The cheap little slut. He acted like butter wouldn't melt in his mouth.

Now they were having sandwiches together. What the fuck would people think if they saw that?

That I'm a mug. That the bastards are taking me for a ride. Not damn likely.

He'd put a stop to this budding romance, sooner rather than later.

Chapter Six

"I see him," Jake shouted from the bow of the boat and raised his hand. "Eleven o'clock."

At the wheel, Dominic Melton adjusted the direction and followed Jake's direction.

They had been out searching for almost half an hour before he'd spotted the casualty. Even today, in mid-July, with the sun shining, every second a person was in the water could be fatal. The North Sea was never warm, not even in summer. They'd been called out for a kayaker who had fallen off his craft and become detached from it. They had found the kayak ten minutes before and hauled it onto the lifeboat before continuing the search for the missing man.

He'd been lucky. A walker had spotted the unmanned kayak from the cliffs at North Point and alerted the coastguard.

Looking for a head above the water was one of the hardest jobs in the lifeboat. In a vast space of open sea, it could be nearly impossible to locate such a tiny figure. Even today, with a modest swell, they could pass by a casualty without ever seeing them.

Dominic eased back on the engines as they gained a better sight and brought the boat up close.

The man in the water looked exhausted. There was desperation and relief on his face as they came alongside. Jake and Minty, the third member of the crew, reached down and hooked the man beneath the armpits. He was a dead weight as they hauled him, first onto the side of the boat, then, with another effort, over into the craft.

"Hey there," Jake said, kneeling in front of the casualty to check his responses. "I'm Jake. Can you tell me your name?"

"R... Ryan," the man said.

Ryan wore a wetsuit, which had likely saved his life. Without it, hypothermia could have claimed him before the boat ever found him.

"Do you know how long you were in the water, Ryan?"

"An hour and a half, I think."

He was talking and responsive. *Great.* "Did you hurt yourself when you went in? Do you have any injuries we should know about?"

"No." Ryan said, shivering.

Minty came in with the blankets and wrapped them around him. Dominic had already turned the boat around and was racing back to the harbour. He radioed ahead to make sure an ambulance would be waiting. The lifeboat crew were trained in first aid, but they were not paramedics. Jake's job now was to sit with Ryan and monitor his level of response. The risk of a casualty going into shock was great once they had been brought on board. He could also have swallowed a lot of water during his time in the sea, and some of it had the potential to make it into his lungs. The crew had to look out for the risk of secondary drowning while getting Ryan safely to the shore.

"How old are you?" Jake asked.

"Fifty-two."

He looked to be in good shape and health, which would have aided his chances of survival.

"What happened to the kayak?"

"A wave," he said. "It came from nowhere, hit me side-on and I capsized. Another one came along straight after and separated me from the boat. I lost both paddles."

"If it makes you feel any better, we've retrieved the kayak. You'll need to fork out for some new paddles, but the kayak is in great shape."

Ryan managed a weak smile, which was another good sign. Jake kept him talking all the way to the harbour and thought he determined a slight improvement in his pallor by the time the boat reached the lifeboat station. An ambulance was waiting, and the paramedics took charge of the casualty.

"Well spotted," Dominic said to Jake as they went inside the station to complete the report and debrief. "It could have been a different outcome if you hadn't seen him when you did."

"It was good luck as much as anything," Jake said, putting on the kettle. It was customary after a rescue for the team to take ten minutes together, to let their adrenaline return to normal levels before heading home.

Dominic sat at the table and made a start on the paperwork. Jake had harboured a crush on Dominic for as long as he'd been volunteering on the crew. It was hard not to. Even some of the straight guys admitted to having a soft spot for him. With his dark hair and moody good looks, he was the sexiest man Jake had ever met, until now. Matt could give Dominic a good run in the hotness department. There was no doubt about that.

Jake checked the time. About eighty minutes had elapsed since the pager had sounded and abruptly cut short their chat. He wondered what Matt was doing now. Could he still be hanging around the marina? It would have been nice to have a drink with him in one of the harbour pubs.

Jake knew where he lived. The house was just a few minutes' walk from the station. There was nothing to stop him from taking a stroll up there and asking Matt out in person.

Bad idea. Jake didn't need to complicate his life any further right now, and that was exactly what Matt would be…a complication. If Vince found out he was interested in Matt, then the shit would really hit the fan. Matt would be gone in a couple of weeks and Jake would still be there, dealing with Vince's crap. No, as tempting as Matt was, Jake had to resist.

He would admire him from afar, like he had with Dominic all these years.

Instead, he sent a quick text to the number Matt had given him, letting him know that the boat had returned safely and the rescue had been a success.

Minty came in just as the kettle reached a boil and Jake made three mugs of tea.

"It looks like the fella will be all right, but they're taking him to the hospital for observation. If everything checks out, he'll be able to go home tonight," Minty said, raiding the cupboard for the biscuit barrel.

"Excellent news," Dominic said, without looking up from the report papers.

Jake left the station just before seven. The marina was still busy with tourists making the most of the warm evening. The Lobster Pot and takeaway restaurants were busy, and the beer gardens of the sea-facing pubs were packed. He considered calling in at one of the bars for a drink on his way home. Monday was his day off — the one morning of the week when he didn't have to get up early.

He decided against it. The forecast for tomorrow was good, so he hoped to take the boat out for a few hours. *Better to go home and get an early night.* If he went to the pub and bumped into anyone he knew, the chances of him staying out until closing time were high.

This freedom was all new, something he'd gained in the last year. Vince had always gone mad if Jake suggested going to the pub with his mates, even the lifeboat crew. Throughout their marriage, Vince had discouraged Jake from making friends. He wanted him home at all times. He'd even been jealous of Lizzie and the café, wanting Jake to turn over his side of the business to her. Vince had tried to exert control over every aspect of Jake's life. It was strange how Jake hadn't noticed just how much he was under Vince's thumb until the dying days of their relationship. For the main part, he'd gone along with whatever Vince had asked of him for the sake of a quiet life.

Vince could be difficult to live with on a good day. When he didn't get what he wanted, he was the worst kind of nightmare.

Jake had walked to work that morning and did the same going home. He preferred to get around the town on foot rather than navigate some of the narrow back streets by car. Walking gave him time to think and clear his head, and he appreciated it even more after being stuck in a hot kitchen for most of the day.

The house he shared with Lizzie was in the newer area of Nyemouth on an estate built in the late nineties. The houses were predominantly semi-detached, each with their own front lawns and rear gardens. When he'd been married, he'd lived in a huge five-bedroom faux-mansion farther out of the town. The house, like everything else, had been Vince's idea, and decorated to his taste. Jake had hated it and couldn't wait to get his half of the property's value in order to start up on his own. His dream would be to live in the old town, up on South Bank Terrace or somewhere in that area. Anywhere close to the sea would suit him.

Lizzie was on the sofa with her girlfriend Kelly when he walked through the front door, her legs stretched over Kelly's lap. They both had bottles of beer in their hands.

"Hi," he called out.

"Hey," Lizzie said. "How did it go? Everyone all right?"

He flopped into the armchair opposite and gave them a quick rundown on the rescue.

"Great job, little brother," Lizzie grinned.

"For sure," Kelly said. "That guy gets to go home safely to his family tonight because of you. You're a hero."

"We're a team. No one on the crew is more important than anyone else."

"I'll still proud of you. It takes real nerve to do what you do."

He laughed. "Maybe. But you know me. I live for the excitement."

"Speaking of excitement," Lizzie said. "Who was that guy you were chatting with when the pager went off?"

Typical Lizzie, she didn't miss a thing. "That was Matt, the guy who intervened in the argument with Vince on Friday."

"Who's this?" Kelly asked, sitting up straighter.

"A guy in the café this afternoon," Lizzie said. "You should have seen him. He looked like a movie star – the tall, dark and handsome type with lovely blue eyes."

"He's here on holiday. I told him to drop by as a thank-you for the other night."

"And?"

"And what? That's it."

She rolled her eyes. "Bullshit. I watched while you were talking to him. Your face was glowing."

"Give over," he protested. "It was not."

"You were drooling," Lizzie screamed. "I thought I was going to have to come over and wipe your chin at one point. It was so obvious you had the hots for him."

Heat rose across his face, and he knew his blushes would give him away. "So what if I did? You said so yourself. He's gorgeous."

"He likes you, too."

"How do you know?" he asked, hoping he didn't sound too desperate.

"I spoke to him. When you ran out the door like a bat out of hell, I came through to see what the hell was wrong. I thought he must have farted or something."

Lizzie and Kelly screeched at the remark. Jake was too wound up to laugh.

"Did you speak to him? What did you say?"

"Relax. I didn't do anything to embarrass you. I just chatted to him for a few minutes, that's all. But I could see from the look on his face that he had the hots for you. He had his back to me when the two of you were talking, but once I got a look at him up close, I could see he was gagging for it as much as you were."

More hilarity from his sister and her girlfriend.

"Don't look so serious," Kelly said to him once they had calmed down.

"Well, stop taking the piss. Nothing happened between us. Nothing *will* happen."

"Oh, c'mon," Lizzie said. "We're just teasing. And don't write the guy off too quickly. He likes you. It's obvious you like him. Why not have a little fun?"

"Oh, maybe a small problem like…I'm married."

"Separated," she corrected. "Big difference. And I mean it. A little fling could do you good. It would certainly cheer you up after years with that arsehole Vince."

"Matt's only here for two weeks," he pointed out.

"That's what makes him perfect for you. You're not signing up for a lifetime together. Have a little fun, a brief romance, some hot times — then go your own way. No ties or commitments. In the entire time you were married to Vince, I never saw you smile the way you did this afternoon with Matt. You looked so happy. You deserve that, Jake. Don't be so down on the idea. A fling with a hot guy like Matt? I think it's exactly what you need."

He shook his head and stood up. "I need a shower. I'm going up."

"Think about it, eh?"

He headed upstairs without a reply. He didn't need his sister to convince him of something he already knew. It was a nice idea, but now was not the time for him. As desirable as Matt was, he would not be part of Jake's future.

Chapter Seven

It was seven-thirty on Tuesday evening when Matt returned to Nyemouth, tired and content after a brilliant day on the coast. He'd driven north late in the morning to the town of Seahouses. With its pretty harbour and cafés, it was very similar to Nyemouth. He'd parked and set off on a three-mile walk along the beach to Bamburgh Castle. It had been a gorgeous afternoon, with bright skies and a refreshing sea breeze. He had lost himself in the beauty of the shoreline and maintained an unhurried pace all the way.

After a light lunch in the village, he'd spent several hours exploring the medieval castle. As it was a weekday, there were fewer tourists around than he'd expected, and he had the freedom to take everything in at leisure. Afterwards he'd stopped at one of the local pubs for a cold beer before starting the return walk to Seahouses, this time along St Oswald's Way, across fields and small country lanes.

It had been a perfect day.

When Matt had been married to Clinton, none of this would have been possible. Clinton couldn't see the point in walking anywhere when he had a flashy car to drive instead. He dismissed places like Seahouses and Bamburgh, devoid of designer shops and trendy bars. Clinton was a city boy with no affection for the countryside or the coast. He would happily bake himself for hours in the sunshine of Marbella, but Matt could never persuade him to check out their English beaches.

"What's the point?" Clinton had moaned when Matt had suggested they spend a Saturday afternoon in Scarborough. *"It'll be fucking freezing. And with all those donkeys on the beaches? No fucking thanks."*

Not even the prospect of arcades filled with slot machines primed to appeal to his gambling instincts had been enough to convince him.

Matt's work colleagues had looked at him with pitiful eyes when they knew he was going on holiday alone. They didn't understand. It was only by himself that he could do the things he wanted to. With anyone else, there would always be compromises to be made. Matt had compromised enough. This was his time to do what the hell he liked.

He arrived back in Nyemouth looking forward to a cool shower, then a takeaway dinner enjoyed on the back patio with a good bottle of red wine. He intended to be in bed by ten-thirty, ready for another busy day tomorrow.

As he drove up South Bank and marvelled once again at the views, he realised how lucky he had been to find this place. It was a lovely, warm night. Maybe he would have his dinner in the front garden instead and make the most of the fantastic views.

He went inside and dumped his backpack at the foot of the stairs, along with his walking boots. As he was about to open the bottle of wine, there was a knock at the front door. He padded back through in his stockinged feet, hoping that whoever this was, they would not keep him long.

He opened the door. It was Jacob, looking smart in cream chinos and a dark polo shirt.

"Hello there," the old man said, cheerful smile in situ. "Sorry to trouble you. I know you've just got home, but I'm heading down to the Mariner's and thought you might be asleep when I got back. I didn't want to miss you."

"It's no trouble." In the last couple of days, Matt had struck up a nice friendship with his neighbour. They'd sat out in the front and enjoyed a cup of coffee this morning just before Matt had set off. "What can I do for you?"

"Oh, it's nothing like that. I thought you ought to know that there was a man here earlier. He was looking for you…around four-thirty."

"Really? Did he say who he was?"

"No. He asked if I knew where you were but wouldn't give his own name. He was a bit surly, if I'm honest. Not the most pleasant of fellas."

"Was it really me he was after? I can't think of anyone who would come looking for me here."

"Yes," Jacob said. "He asked for you by name."

Matt couldn't imagine who would track him down to Nyemouth. He'd kept his phone on him the whole time. If an emergency had arisen on one of his cases, the guys at the office could have reached him on that. They wouldn't have had to come looking for him. "What did he look like?"

"Oh, God. I'm not very good at this. He was probably your age, maybe a year or two older. Quite flashy looking. Fancy clothes, if you know what I mean. He was thickset, heavy around the middle. What else? He had dark hair but short, going thin on top. A very heavy suntan, like he'd just come back from holiday."

Matt groaned.

Jacob's smile wavered. "What is it? Someone who shouldn't be here?"

"You could say that. Did he wear a lot of gold jewellery? Chunky bracelets, heavy rings."

"Erm, not that I really noticed. Maybe a ring, but I didn't spot anything else."

No surprise. He's probably sold them or lost them in a bet.

"It sounds like my ex-husband." Matt pulled his phone from his pocket and brought up the picture gallery, scrolling until he found a photo of Clinton. He showed the screen to Jacob. "This is a few years old, but is that him?"

"Yes. That's the man."

"Shit."

"I take it he's not welcome?"

Matt shook his head. "I don't know how he even knew to find me here. One of our mutual friends has obviously blabbed." He gave a long, drawn-out sigh. "I came here hoping for a bit of peace. It didn't last long."

"Is he bad news? Do you want me to do anything if he shows his face again?"

"No. It's fine. Thanks for the forewarning. It would have been a bigger shock if I'd opened the door to find him there. At least now I'll be prepared. Thanks, Jacob."

"It's no problem. Did you have a good day?"

"I did. Perfect, in fact." Matt told him about his walk along the coast.

"That's good. I'm glad to hear you enjoyed it. Well, I best be going. The quiz starts at eight but Peter, one of the guys on my team, gets himself in a bother if we're not all there by a quarter to. Have a good night."

"You too," Matt said, stepping back inside.

Clinton. What the hell was he doing here? It didn't take Matt long to come up with the answer — looking for money. Another bailout. *The nerve of the man to follow me all the way to Nyemouth.* He must have put pressure on one of their friends to know which house he was staying in. It was an imposition too far.

Matt went back to the kitchen, poured a glass of wine and sat down with his phone. There was no point in prolonging this. The last thing he wanted was a return visit from his ex. He dialled Clinton's number.

"Hey, Matt," he answered after just one ring. "Great to hear from you. How are you doing?" His voice was relaxed and breezy, as though he hadn't spent the afternoon staking out Matt's holiday home.

"I'm fine, Clinton, just fine," he said wearily. "But a more important question is, what were you doing here today?"

"Ah, the old dude told you I dropped by, did he?"

"It sounded like you were as subtle as a brick. What do you want? As if I don't know."

"Don't be so pissy. I was in the area and dropped by to see you."

Matt rolled his eyes and took a drink. This was always a problem with Clinton, even when he begged a favour — having to wade through the bullshit to discover what he wanted. "You were in Northumberland at the same time I'm on holiday here. That's a coincidence and a half, don't you think?"

"Ha-ha. Only you would take a holiday to the arse-end of nowhere. That house... Oh my God, couldn't you have found a nice hotel to stay in? Why are you slumming it in that old dump?"

"I'm trying to relax, and that's something you're not helping with. So, come on and stop wasting my time. What are you after? Or, more to the point, how much?"

Clinton chuckled. "It sounds like you do need to relax. Man, are you uptight. That's what happens when you stay in a dreary fishing village. You wouldn't be like this if you'd gone to Spain and got some sun on your skin."

"Clinton," he snapped.

"All right, all right, calm your tits. You can be mean at times, you know that? You've been ignoring my texts. I had no choice but to come find you."

"I'm not giving you the two grand you want, if that's what this is about. You've had enough money from me."

Clinton gave a big huff down the phone. "Two grand. Fuck, if that's all it was. I'm in a hole, Matt. I wouldn't come to you unless I was desperate."

"How much of a hole?"

"Twenty thousand. If I don't pay up by Thursday, it goes up to twenty-five."

"Fucking hell, Clinton, who do you owe the money to?"

"The wrong kind of people."

Matt had heard rumours from friends that, since losing his job, Clinton had spiralled further out of control, and that he spent on drugs and gambling like he was still earning a good wage. "What about Sonny? Can't he help you out?"

"Sonny's gone. He left when the knocks at the door became more persistent. It frightened him off."

Matt hadn't seen Sonny—Clinton's latest boyfriend—in person, but he'd heard from friends that he was a twenty-one-year-old ambitious social media star. They said he'd taken one look at Clinton with his clothes, car and jewellery, and thought he was a man who could keep him in the lifestyle he aspired to. Someone had shown Matt Sonny's Instagram account, which in the beginning had been filled with photos of them on holiday, enjoying cocktails, champagne and sunsets. The dumb kid hadn't understood that Clinton's lavish existence was funded by a string of increasingly maxed-out credit cards. At least he'd had the sense to get out before any real harm was done.

"Clinton, I can't help you."

"Oh, c'mon. Don't say that. You're the only person I can ask now. Please, Matt, for old times' sake. I wouldn't come to you if I weren't desperate."

"Clinton, I've lost count of the money you already owe me. I don't expect to get any of that back now, but I can't give you any more."

"I will pay you back, every penny and more. I promise I will. I just need you to help me now."

"I can't," he said, exasperated. "I'm not a bank. I don't have that kind of money to give."

"Don't have the money? You're loaded. I know you are. You've got loads of cash put aside."

He took a deep breath, determined not to be pressured into anything. "All my money is invested. I can't get at it just like that, and even if I could, I'm not giving you twenty thousand pounds. I know you, Clinton. You won't pay off your debts. You'll gamble it away, thinking you're going to make big on the outlay."

"Not anymore. I need to pay these guys off this week. I have no choice."

Matt remained firm. "The answer is no. You've wasted thousands and thousands in the years I've known you. I walked away from all that when I left you. I'm not taking money out of my investment savings for you to piss it all up the wall again. That money is for my future, not your drug debts."

Clinton wouldn't be put off that easily. "How about a loan?"

"What have I just said? *No*."

"I don't mean your money. You could take out a bank loan and let me pay it off. I can't get any credit, but a bank would loan you that amount in minutes. You could fill out an application right now and have the cash by tomorrow."

Matt laughed, despite his shock. "You've got to be joking, except I know you're not. I'm sorry, Clinton, but you got yourself into this mess and you must get yourself out. I can't help you. Ask your parents or your sister. If they know how bad it is, I'm sure they'll oblige, but I don't owe you a thing. Our marriage is over, and I've given you all I'm ever going to already. Now don't call me again, and don't come looking for me, because the answer will still be no. Goodnight."

Matt hung up, and before Clinton could call him back, he switched off the phone. His hands trembled. One phone call had undone all the good his day at the coast had achieved.

Chapter Eight

A sudden buzzing noise from the bedside table woke Jake. He'd been in a deep sleep, but his eyes shot open. In an instant he flung back the covers and swept his legs over the side, already reaching for the light switch. Instinct told him it was another lifeboat call, and he had to move fast. As his senses came into focus, he realised the noise was not the loud alarm of his pager but his mobile phone. He glanced at the time as he reached for the device. It had just gone two a.m.

He looked at the caller ID and was suddenly wide awake. Castle Alarms, the security firm that ran the system for the café.

"Hello," he answered, stifling a yawn.

"This is Mary from Castle Intruder Security. May I speak with Mr Jake Wrangler?"

"That's me," he said, getting to his feet, stumbling to the dresser for socks and underpants. The caller asked him for the unique password, which he struggled to remember at that hour. "It's, er…Eldorado."

Satisfied, Mary proceeded. "I regret to inform you that the intruder alarm has been triggered at the Seagull Café in Nyemouth marina. I have already informed the police, sir."

"When?"

"The alarm went off five minutes ago."

"Thanks," he said. "I'm on my way."

Jake hung up and stepped into his underpants. He pulled on last night's jeans and T-shirt and his Converse shoes. It was probably a false alarm, but they required one of the key holders to attend to deactivate the security system. He crept across the hall and tried to make his way downstairs in the dark.

"Jake," Lizzie called from her bedroom. The door was ajar. "What is it? A lifeboat shout?"

"The alarm has gone off at the café. I'm going to check it out."

"I'll come with you."

"There's no need. I'm already up. I'll be halfway there before you even get dressed. It's fine. Go back to sleep."

"No, I'll follow you down."

There was no point in arguing. Lizzie would do what she wanted.

The streets were deserted, and he drove from the estate to the marina in less than five minutes. As he turned the corner to the front of the café, he saw the blue lights of a police car parked right outside. The alarm was still ringing.

Jake jumped out of the car and identified himself to the two police officers, a man and a woman around his own age. The full-length windows at the front of the shop had been broken.

"It looks like criminal damage," the female officer told him, "but if you shut off the alarm, you can tell us if anything is missing."

Jake nodded and hurried inside, being careful where he stepped. Glass crunched under his feet. The alarm box was located just behind the counter. He went around and switched it off. The sudden silence was as startling as the noise. Jake let out a long breath and turned on the lights.

His spirits sank as he turned around to assess the damage. It wasn't just the windows that were broken. Whoever had done it had hurled an open tin of red paint inside. It was all over the first few tables, the floor and up the walls.

Bastards.

"This doesn't look like a standard case of criminal damage," the police officer said, identifying herself as PCSO Shah.

"No," Jake said, his depression deepening as he took in the full extent of the paint splatter.

"Usually it's some drunk falling against a window and breaking it — or a couple of lads fighting, and one pushes the other too hard. This" — she swept her hand across the paint splashes — "is deliberate."

"It looks that way, doesn't it?"

"First things first... Let's see if anything is missing, eh?"

There was a small office off the kitchen where the money was locked away. He led the police officer through. "Very little cash is kept on the premises," he explained. "I usually bank the day's takings each afternoon."

No one had been back here. The cupboard containing the safe was locked, and there had been no attempt to force it.

"What about supplies?" PCSO Shah asked. "Anything valuable in there someone might want to take?"

"Let's see."

They went along to the stock room and freezers, but it was obvious straight away that nothing had been touched.

"So, it's just the windows and the paint," she said. "What about CCTV? Do you have any cameras covering the front of the café?"

"Sure," he said, "back in the office." As he turned on the monitor and programmed the system to show him everything from one-fifty a.m. onward, he wondered who would want to target them. If it were just the windows, he would put the blame on mischievous kids, but the paint suggested a more personal attack. Someone wanted to cause greater disruption than a few panes of broken glass.

"Have you had any incidents with your customers lately? Something that might cause someone to hold a grudge?"

He cast his mind back all summer and couldn't recall a single wrong word with any of the customers, neither their regulars nor passing trade. "We're not the kind of place that gets a lot of aggro," he said. "People come in for a breakfast roll or a light lunch, and we don't get any trouble. I'll check with my sister in case I missed anything, but if something had occurred, she would have told me…at great length."

He watched the screen. The camera was fixed at the rear of the dining room, covering the entire floor and front window. As the clock came up to two a.m., he saw movement on the other side. He sat forward in his chair to watch closely.

It happened in seconds. A figure appeared at the window and took a swing, and the first panel of glass imploded. The person moved like lightning to the next pane, shattering it with a long implement that looked like a hammer or a mallet. The third panel of glass went next, then the open tin of paint came flying inside, spilling its contents everywhere. Then the figure was gone. The whole incident lasted seconds.

"The bastard," Jake cursed. The action was so blatantly malicious.

"Can you take that back again?" the police officer asked. "It looks like they are wearing a mask of some kind, but I'd like another look."

Jake did as she'd asked, and when he replayed the footage, he zoomed in on the figure. They were dressed entirely in black with a balaclava over their face. It was hard to make out any details. They looked average height and build.

PCSO Shah spoke into her radio. "Can you take a look up and down the street just to see if they have targeted any other properties in the area?"

"I have," her colleague replied. "That's negative. The café is the only target."

Jake shook his head. In the whole time he'd been living in Nyemouth, he'd been unaware of a similar situation. He had no enemies. None that he knew of. No one who would do something like this.

Apart from Vince.

He found it hard to believe. Would his ex really have trashed the place? What would he have gained from it, besides the inconvenience it would cause? He knew what Lizzie would say. Vince didn't need any other reason than getting back at him. Jake knew all the ways his husband had tried to control him in the past. He'd even wanted him to give up the business.

But broken windows and paint? Not even he could be so petty. *Could he?*

The answer was yes…undoubtedly. If he thought it would hurt him, Vince would try anything.

Jake looked at the figure on the screen again. Was that Vince under the balaclava? From the high angle, he couldn't tell.

It could be anyone.

Jake heard voices outside. Lizzie and Kelly had arrived.

"That's my sister and business partner," he explained to the police officer.

"Let's see if she has any theories?" PCSO Shah said with a smile.

Kelly had her arm around Lizzie's shoulder when they went back through to the dining room. Her face was slack with shock.

"Have they taken anything?" she asked.

He shook his head. "They've trashed the place. Nothing else. They made off as soon as they'd lobbed the paint through."

"I asked your brother if you've had any trouble lately," PCSO Shah asked. "Irritated customers? A member of staff you had to let go? Anyone with something to be pissed about?"

Lizzie looked at Jake. "Nothing. We've had no trouble in years."

"That's what I thought," he said. "No even a quibble over a bill."

"But someone was pissed off enough to do this," Kelly said.

Lizzie still looked at Jake. He knew what was coming next.

"Vince," she said.

"I don't think so. He wouldn't."

"Who else would? He's nuts enough. And we know he's got a temper on him."

"Who is Vince?" the police officer asked.

"He's my husband. We're separated. But I don't think he's capable of something on this scale."

"You'd be surprised," PCSO Shah said, pulling out her notebook. "Let me have the details and we'll check him out just the same."

"I don't think—"

"Jake," Lizzie cut him off, "he hit you less than a week ago. If he can do that, he's more than capable of breaking our windows. The man is a psycho, and he can't stand losing. He's not going to stop until he gets his own way. And I'm pretty sure that means hurting you in any way he can."

He thought his sister was being overly dramatic, but it was obvious she intended to tell the police about Vince, whether he liked it or not. With a sigh, he gave the officer Vince's details.

Chapter Nine

Jacob told Matt about the vandalism at The Seagull. He had just returned from a pre-breakfast run along the clifftops and encountered his neighbour coming home from a trip into town to buy a newspaper and fresh milk.

"Someone has made a real mess of the place," Jacob said. "There's red paint everywhere. It has taken them hours to clean up. Jake and Lizzie have been there for most of the night."

"Who would do such a shitty thing?" Matt asked.

"I can hazard a good guess," Jacob said.

"Vince?"

"It's got to be. Spiteful, malicious, petty... It's got his name all over it, I'd say."

Matt went inside to take a shower, but his thoughts were preoccupied with Jake and Vince throughout. Vince wouldn't be the first jilted partner he'd known of who resorted to meaningless criminal damage to get back at a spouse. Anything with personal meaning to their exes was fair game to people like that. Cars were often the first thing they targeted, but homes and workplaces came a close second and third.

In his experience, things could turn even nastier when there were children involved. Parental responsibility often came second to revenge, and they would use their kids in the most brutal way to get back at another parent. It was the most disturbing aspect of his job, dealing with mothers and fathers who used their offspring as weapons against each other.

Luckily, Jake and Vince had no children to get caught up in their battles.

Showered and dressed, Matt couldn't stop thinking about Jake. He'd tried his hardest to forget him these last few days, but it had been impossible. He hadn't found a single distraction that had kept him from his thoughts for more than a few hours.

It didn't matter what he did or where he went. He couldn't help wondering what it would be like if Jake was with him.

Unable to resist any longer, he got out his phone and sent Jake a text.

I heard what happened. Hope you are okay. If you need any help, let me know.

He had just filled the kettle when his phone rang.

"Hi," Jake said. "Thanks for getting in touch. That was kind of you."

"Are you all right?"

"Not bad," he said, though he sounded weary. "We've been here all night, but we're almost done cleaning up. The new windows are being fitted now. Have you got half an hour to spare? I could do with a coffee."

Matt brightened in an instant. "Sure. Do you want me to meet you there?"

"No. I need a break from this place. Is it okay if I meet you at your place? The walk up and fresh air will do me good. I'll be there in five minutes, if it's okay with you?"

"Perfect. I'll see you soon."

Despite the promise that he'd made not to get involved with Jake, Matt experienced a rush of euphoria knowing they were about to meet. Was there any point in resisting his feelings when they were so strong? Surely it would be better to give in to them.

No. There were two powerful reasons why Matt and Jake were no good for each other right now — Vince and Clinton. *The toxic exes.*

Those men were too involved in each of their lives. This was not the time to complicate the situation further.

Matt scrambled some eggs and had just finished eating when Jake arrived. When he opened the door, he was shocked at the man's appearance. He hadn't seen him look so dishevelled. His skin was pale, which only deepened the shadows under his eyes.

"I know," Jake said, stepping inside. "I look terrible. I think I managed a couple of hours' sleep last night before the rude awakening."

"You still look good to me," Matt said, triggering Jake's beautiful smile. "Come through. I take it you want coffee."

"Yes, please. As strong as you can make it."

They went into the kitchen. Matt swept his breakfast plates from the table and into the sink. He grabbed Jake a mug from the cupboard and added a spoon and a half of instant coffee. It would taste disgusting, but the poor guy looked like he needed the lift. "Milk? Sugar?"

"Ordinarily, yes to both, but today I'll take it black."

Matt opened the doors to the rear garden. "Let's go outside."

It was another fine morning for their far-north location. Though he had only been here a few days so far, he realised he had really lucked out on the weather. The back terrace didn't see the benefit of any direct sunlight during the day, but it was so sheltered that as long as it stayed dry, it was a lovely place to sit at any time of day.

As Jake dropped onto the sofa, Matt noticed the tips of his fingers were stained red from the vandal's paint.

"How bad is the interior?" he asked.

"We've got the worst of it up now. There are just a couple of chairs left to clean. You wouldn't think a regular tin of paint could spread to so many places."

"How long will you have to stay closed?"

"Our staff are going to open the doors around eleven. It won't be a full menu today, because I intend to go home to bed after one, but we can serve sandwiches and stuff like that."

Matt didn't know why Jake's resilience came as a surprise. This was a man who took part in high-sea rescues in his spare time. A few broken windows wouldn't stop him.

"Any ideas about who did it?"

"Besides my psycho husband?" he asked with a weary smile.

"Is that what you think happened?"

"Everybody else does. Vince is the number one suspect. He called me this morning, full of concern when he heard the news—except he's in Amsterdam.

He flew out for work yesterday and won't be back until tonight. So, he couldn't have done it himself if he was out of the country, but Lizzie says that doesn't mean a thing. Vince doesn't like to get his hands dirty, so if he were responsible, he'd have paid someone to do it for him."

"Is that likely?"

He sighed. "It wouldn't be impossible. Put it that way. He has a lot of people who work for him in the warehouse. There will be plenty of guys prepared to do what the boss asks them to for a nice tax-free back-hander."

"But is it likely he would do that to you? He's trying to get you back, isn't he? Trashing your business would be a strange way to go about it."

"Vince has a lot of strange ways. I can't plead his case to Lizzie because I know better than anyone what he's capable of doing." He took a sip of coffee before continuing. "Vince is a control freak. At work, at home, he has to be in charge of everything, all the time, otherwise he loses it. I think the longer I stay away from him, the more out of control he feels. I'm beginning to think Lizzie is right, and I wouldn't put anything past him now."

A sadness came over his face as he spoke — the kind of look Matt had seen so often on the faces of his clients as they gradually came to terms with the years they had wasted in a dysfunctional relationship. Matt had been there himself. He knew how much it hurt.

"Have you told the police about your suspicions? If this is the beginning of an escalation in Vince's behaviour, the sooner they log the incidents, the easier it will be to take action against him, should it come to that."

"Lizzie saw to that. She told them everything, including all the details about Friday night."

"That's good," Matt said.

"I told them I didn't want to make a complaint."

"It won't matter. The fact that they know about it means they'll log it on their system as a domestic incident. If anything else happens that leads to Vince's arrest, it will show up in his history."

Jake straightened in alarm. "Arrest? I don't want him arrested. I don't want to get him in any trouble."

"You won't," Matt said soothingly. "If anyone gets Vince in trouble with the police, it will be Vince. Vandalising property and assaulting his husband? That's all on him and no one else."

Jake slumped back on the sofa. "We don't know he's behind the broken windows."

"But what are the chances?" Matt asked.

Jake sighed. "Pretty high."

"There you go, then. Don't worry about causing any trouble for him. It looks to me like he can do that all by himself."

At last, Jake smiled. It was still kind of sad and filled with weary emotion, but it was good to see some humour coming through. "Sorry," he said. "You're supposed to be on holiday and I'm ruining it for you with all my personal drama."

"You're not ruining anything," Matt said. He meant it. "I'm glad I met you."

The words lingered in the air. They were magical, filled with potential. Then Jake said, "I'm glad we met too." He sipped his coffee and said, "You know... I've been so caught up in my own shit that I haven't once asked you anything about yourself. What do you do,

Matt? When you're not helping out strangers in distress."

"I'm a lawyer," he said.

Jake's hand flew to his mouth. "You're kidding."

"No. It's true."

"Oh my God, I'm so sorry. This just makes it even worse. You come away for a break and you get involved in the kind of mess you must have to deal with every other day. That's no kind of holiday."

"Relax," he said. "You haven't spoiled a thing."

A pink colour rose in Jake's cheeks. "I should have known. I wondered whether you were involved with the police, seeing how you knew so much about their processes and arrest procedures, but you being a lawyer all makes perfect sense. I'm so embarrassed. It's like I've been pestering you for free advice."

Matt found Jake's blushes completely endearing. "Don't worry about a thing. I've been in your situation and understand what you're going through."

"You do?"

"Sure. The circumstances were different, but the emotional turmoil is just the same. My husband wasn't like Vince, but he had a lot of other problems. It's a long story I'll save for another day, I don't want to rehash it all now, but things will get better. It probably doesn't feel like it now, especially this morning, but you'll get through it and be a lot stronger for it."

Jake fixed him with those deep blue eyes, so sparkling and pure in the morning light. "How long were you married?"

"About the same as you and Vince. Four years."

"Do you regret it? Getting married?"

"No. Not at all. I loved Clinton at the time, and it seemed like the right thing to do. I just didn't know him as well as I thought I did. He kept a lot of things hidden from me. I would only have regretted it if I'd stayed in a bad marriage for longer than I did."

"It sounds like you have it all figured out. How are things now? Between you and Clinton?"

Matt laughed. "Not as final as I'd like. Our divorce is through, but he still feels like he can hit me up for cash whenever he runs into trouble."

"How long has it been?"

"Four years again."

"Shit. The idea that Vince could still be a major part of my life after so long doesn't bear thinking about."

"Then try not to think about it. There's nothing to say he will. Every divorce is different."

There was so much hope in Jake's eyes that it caused something to tighten deep inside Matt. He couldn't control the growing affection he had for this boy.

"It's crap, isn't it?" Jake said. "The two of us are here alone, and we've spent the whole time talking about the men we *don't* want to be with."

"It is kind of strange," he admitted.

Jake put down the mug and leaned forward. "Look… This could be the exhaustion causing me to do things I wouldn't otherwise dare to, but I really like you, Matt. And I don't want to put my life on hold while I wait for Vince to sign some papers. Can we start over? I'd like to go out, just the two of us. We could go to some of the local pubs. I'll take you for a nice meal at The Lobster Pot to make up for all the help you've given me. How about it? Are you interested?"

His words came out in a rush. Matt took a moment to catch on to what he was saying. When he did, his answer was immediate.

"I'd love to."

Jake brightened even further. "You would?"

"Absolutely." He'd been denying how much he wanted Jake since the moment they'd met. Why should he hold back any longer? Jake was right. They'd wasted too much time worrying about the previous men in their lives. It was time to think about each other. "You need to catch up on your sleep and get some rest. How about tomorrow night?"

"The wait is going to kill me," Jake answered. "But you're on."

Chapter Ten

Despite being kept busy by well-wishing customers and a hectic day in the kitchen, Jake couldn't remember time ever passing so slowly. Waiting for his date with Matt to come around was as bad as Christmas Eve to an eight-year-old. His focus kept wandering to the clock, and it flooded him with disappointment to realise only minutes had passed since the last time he'd looked. The day seemed like it would never end.

Lizzie didn't miss his distraction. "What's got into you today?" she asked when he sent out a roast beef sandwich for a customer who had ordered tuna.

"Nothing," he said, avoiding her penetrating stare.

"Nothing, my arse. You've had a goofy grin on your face since I came in this morning—which is kind of strange, considering what happened yesterday, don't you think? And that's the third order you've mixed up in the last hour. So, come on, spill the tea. What is it that's got you acting so scatter-brained?"

Typical Lizzie. She knew him far too well.

He looked around, making sure there was no one else in earshot. While Vince would find out soon enough, Jake didn't want him to hear about his date with Matt until it was over. "I'm going out after work tonight. Keep it to yourself, though. Not a word to any of the customers."

Now she smiled, her face lighting up in glee. "Going out…as in a date?"

He nodded.

"Oh my God," she squealed. "About time. Is it that cute guy who came in the other day? The one you were talking to?"

"His name is Matt. And yes, it's him."

"That's fantastic. Where are you going?"

"I said I'd meet him in The Fisherman's Arms for a drink at seven, then we'll go to The Lobster Pot for dinner."

Lizzie came rushing across the kitchen and wrapped her arms around him. "I'm so happy for you."

"Hey, it's just a date with a visiting stranger. Let's not get too excited."

"It's a lot more than that," she said. "It's not about Matt. It's about you. You're moving on, and this is another huge step forward, leaving that prick Vince far behind in the dust. It's what tonight symbolises almost as much as the date itself. But I'll compliment you on your good taste too. Matt is mighty fine. You've certainly improved in your choices."

"Well, we both know Vince is going to go ape-shit when he hears about it, so let's keep it from him for a long as possible, lest we get the new windows smashed in."

"Ah, so you've come round to my way of thinking on that. He's definitely behind what happened here."

"There's no evidence, but he seems the most likely suspect. I can't think of anyone else who would want to do that to us."

"That's because there *is* no one else. But you're right. You do need to be careful. Isn't there somewhere else you and Matt can go this evening? Get out of town for the night. That way there'll be even less chance of Vince finding out."

"I considered that, but I don't want to. Nyemouth is my home. If I let him drive me out of it, then it's another win for him, don't you think? I want to take Matt out and show him all the town has to offer. Besides, Vince won't be here tonight. He looks down his nose at Nyemouth. He thinks the people and bars are tacky. There's no chance we'll run into him."

"No, but one of his lackies is sure to report back to him," she said. "Kelly is working tonight. I'll ask her to put you in one of those nice booths at the back of the restaurant. There's less chance of you being spied on there."

"I'm already ahead of you. I called them yesterday and requested a table at the back."

"Good thinking. Now, I'll take the early shift here in the morning. You come in as late as you like."

"You don't have to do that. I wake up early anyway."

"In your own little bed," she said. "Tonight, you need to keep your options wide open. You might not be so keen to jump up at the crack of dawn tomorrow. And, can I add, I'll be very disappointed if you do."

* * * *

At last, three-thirty arrived and Jake knocked off work. Lizzie gave him another hug and a kiss and wished him well for the evening ahead. He left the café by the back door. They were still busy out front, and he didn't want to get delayed by the well-meaning customers.

The trashing of the venue was still major news among their regulars, and everyone wanted to have their say.

Jake slung the backpack containing his work clothes over his shoulder and headed up the street. It was another wonderful day, and he hoped the good weather would hold until tonight. It would be nice if he and Matt could enjoy a couple of beers, maybe even a cocktail on one of the outdoor terraces, before going in for their meal. When the weather was as good as this, Nyemouth could complete with any of the lush towns in the south of France or Spain.

Jake wondered what he should wear and wished he'd had time to go shopping for a shirt. He couldn't remember when he'd last bought anything new. Maybe around Christmas last year, but that wouldn't be right for a mild summer evening. He had plenty of light, short-sleeved shirts, but they were all so old.

Then again, Matt hadn't struck him as a fashion-conscious guy. Although everything he wore was well-fitted and of good quality, it had all been basic and functional. Jake shelved his concerns. He had lots of good clothes in his wardrobe, and he was sure Matt would appreciate him just the way he was.

Unlike Vince. Vince had spent the last few years of their marriage trying to improve Jake — or, rather, mould him into the kind of man he thought he should be. Vince disapproved of Jake's choice of clothes and would buy him the boring designer T-shirts and jeans he liked to wear himself. Vince criticised most of the things Jake liked, from food to movies and music. He would laugh and belittle all the stuff Jake was into. Jake had been allowed no input into their home. Vince had chosen all the furniture, wallpaper and paint. If Jake brought home something he liked, such as a cushion or a house plant, it would vanish after a few days of grumbling from Vince. It had been like living in a cage most of the time—a luxurious, well-appointed, utterly stifling cage.

It was only now, looking back from a distance, that he could see how bad it had been. When he was caught up inside it, it had just been part of life.

Not anymore, he thought, bouncing brightly up the path to the estate. Whether or not Vince wanted to sign the divorce papers, that was all behind him. Moving in with Lizzie had been the first step towards a new life without him. Now, tonight, his first date since his teenage years, he was truly starting anew.

Every time he thought about Matt, Jake experienced a pleasurable, tingling sensation inside, unlike anything he'd ever known before. He knew for sure he'd never felt this way about Vince, not even in the early days of their relationship. Vince had been more like an older brother to him—a kindly figure who'd provided him with support when he'd needed it the most. At least that was how it had seemed. Jake was wiser now, wise enough to see that Vince had taken advantage of him when he had been at his lowest point. To lose his mother, the one stable figure in his whole life, had been devastating. The world had suddenly seemed terrifying. Vince had provided a shield from all that. He'd presented himself almost as a surrogate father figure, and Jake had latched on to him.

It wasn't all Vince's fault. Jake knew he was just as culpable for the failures in their relationship. He'd grabbed on to Vince because he'd needed him at the time, when a deep part of him had known that it wasn't right. He's spent years trying to make it so, but it wasn't to be.

They were not meant for each other.

Jake had no expectations about what might happen with Matt, other than they'd spend a lovely night together and enjoy each other's company. From what Matt had told him yesterday, he had his own history of dodgy relationships and would probably be very cautious about starting something new. Maybe it would turn out to be nothing more than a holiday flirtation.

Jake could live with that.

He could do with a little flirting.

As he turned into the cul-de-sac, his heart sank.

Vince's car was parked outside the house.

With no back route to the property, there was no way to avoid him.

Damn it. Jake lifted his chin, determined to keep this as brief as possible, whatever Vince intended.

Vince got out of the car as he approached. Jake already had the key to the front door in his hand.

Vince, dressed in a light grey suit, must have come from work.

"Hello, stranger," he said, stepping onto the path in front of Jake.

"Unless you've come to tell me you've signed those divorce documents, I haven't got time for this."

"Well, that's a charming welcome," he said with exaggerated civility, "considering you sent the police round to the warehouse this morning. You do know all of my staff saw them arrive to question me."

"I'm sure it's all part of their enquiries."

"I told them what I told you," he said, all smarmy fake charm. "I was in Amsterdam when your café was trashed. I've got the plane tickets and hotel receipts to prove it."

"Maybe they should have questioned some of your staff while they were there," Jake said, refusing to fall for his intimidation tactics.

Vince let out a larger-than-life laugh. "And what that's supposed to mean?"

"Exactly what it sounds like. You might not have done the job yourself, but I'm sure there are plenty of people in the warehouse who would have done it for you, no questions asked."

"Wow, paranoid much? You've been spending too much time with that bitch sister of yours. You're starting to sound like her."

"Well, in referenced to what I said first, you're not here about the divorce, so we're done. Go back to work, Vince. You're wasting your time here." Jake stepped around him.

Vince shot his hand out and grabbed his elbow. "Not so fucking fast. You can't really think you can send the police my way, and that will be the end. To *embarrass* me like that, in front of all those people who look up to me? Do you know how disrespectful that is?"

Jake knew better than to rise to his provocation. If Vince saw he was getting a reaction, he would twist the knife further. Jake kept his voice very level and calm, the way he'd heard Matt speak to Vince on Friday. "I'd say it's as respectful as smashing up a café out of spite. That's the kind of thing I'd expect from a stroppy fourteen-year-old with a massive chip on his shoulder."

Vince frowned and the oily façade faded. Jake saw in an instant that he'd struck a nerve, and any lingering doubt he'd had about Vince's innocence vanished. He was responsible for the damage, all right, no matter how much he denied it.

"Well, well, well," Vince said. "When did you grow a pair of balls? The boy who used to cry himself to sleep… The boy who was no one when I met him… You were nothing, you know? Just a poor little bastard with no grace. I'm the one who dragged you out of the gutter and made something of you, and you've got the nerve to tell me I've got a chip on my shoulder. What the actual fuck? That's your bitch sister talking again. You wouldn't have dared answer me back before you moved in with that cunt."

Jake jerked his arm away. "And, with that insult, we're finally done. Get back in your car and piss off. I don't want to see you around here or at the café ever again. If I do, then I'll apply for a restraining order to keep you out of my life for good."

Vince roared with laughter. "A restraining order? Who the hell do you think you are?"

"I'm someone who's put up with your abuse for far too long," Jake said, his nerves tingling. It was quite an elation to stand up to him at last. No more tiptoeing around, scared to say anything that might offend him. "We're finished. I'm moving on. The sooner you do the same, the happier we'll all be."

Vince stiffened. "Moving on? What's that supposed to mean?"

Jake stepped around him, already walking up the path to the front door. "Goodbye, Vince."

"You're fucking someone else," Vince shouted. "I knew it, you slut. You wouldn't leave me of your own accord. Of course there had to be someone else. Christ. How long has it been going on, eh? How many years have you been making a mug of me?"

Jake ignored him and stepped into the house.

"Tell me," Vince screamed. "Tell me who it is, you whore."

Jake shut the door and locked it. Once secure, his legs weakened and the muscle of his thighs trembled. He sat on the stairs and took several deep breaths.

Vince wouldn't take this without a fight. Jake knew him better than that, but at least now he might finally accept that their marriage was over for good.

There would be no going back.

Chapter Eleven

Matt didn't leave the house until five minutes to seven. He'd been ready since six-thirty but didn't want to get there too early. He'd poured a double shot of the dark rum he'd bought at the local shop, given it a splash of Diet Coke and drank it in the front garden, watching the low evening sun sparkle on the calm sea and create the most beautiful shades of blue, violet and gold upon its surface. The rum went some way to calming his nerves.

It wasn't an unpleasant sensation — more excitement than apprehension — but he'd been feeling it all day, and it had grown stronger in the last two hours. He didn't know why the prospect of a date with Jake made him react that way. He'd been with other guys since Clinton. There'd been three short-term relationships and a couple of casual hook-ups. It wasn't the idea of a going on a date that got to him. It was going on a date with Jake.

This young guy had really gotten under his skin in the short time Matt had known him.

The Fisherman's Arms was in the harbour, right on the waterfront, just a few minutes' walk from the house. Matt arrived exactly on time.

His stomach churned as he went inside. The interior was traditional old world, with wood-panelled walls and low ceilings. He didn't imagine it had altered much in the last hundred years. He looked around for Jake. There were a lot of tiny rooms and alcoves in the pub, places where people could lose themselves. There was no sign of him inside. Matt stepped out onto the terrace which overlooked the harbour. It was a glorious evening, and it was much busier outside than in. He continued his search.

Jake stood from a table right on the waterfront and waved.

Oh, wow, he's stunning.

Matt approached, beaming. Jake looked incredible. He wore a dark blue short-sleeved shirt and light chinos. The late-in-the-day sun cast a golden hue over his handsome features and made the glossy waves in his hair shine. Those dimples cut deep into his cheeks as he returned Matt's heartfelt smile.

"Great to see you," Jake said.

He put his hand gently on Matt's waist and leaned in to plant soft kisses on each cheek. He smelled wonderfully fresh, wearing a light fragrance Matt didn't recognise.

"You too," he replied. All his prior nerves evaporated now that they were together. "Have you been waiting long?"

"About ten minutes," Jake answered. "I got here early to ensure we snagged a table on the terrace. Even then, I was lucky."

"Let me get you something to drink? What will you have?"

"I'll have a pint of dark fruit cider, please."

"Be right back."

Matt let out a long exhalation as he waited at the bar, still unsure of why he'd been nervous about tonight. It was unlikely Jake would have stood him up, seeing how the date had been his suggestion. *It's because you like him...really like him.* More than anyone he could remember.

He'd always been wary of getting involved with younger men and realised that was also part of his worry. He'd believed men of different ages could have little in common besides sexual attraction. What did they talk about when they were out of bed? He was about to find out. Not that he had many concerns about Jake on that front. He seemed wise beyond his years. An old soul. *It's not like the age gap between us is huge,* he told himself. About fourteen years. It was nothing, really.

For me, perhaps. For Jake, that's more than half his life. Jesus, he probably thinks I'm ancient.

Doubt threatened to creep back in. Matt batted it aside and ordered their drinks. He'd never tried the dark fruit cider Jake had asked for, but as he watched the bar tender pour the rich, purple-coloured pint, he ordered one for himself too.

Jake was waiting, a welcoming smile still plastered on his face, when Matt returned to the terrace and slipped into the seat opposite him.

"Cheers," he said, raising his glass.

"Cheers," Jake answered, clinking glasses. "Here's to a great evening ahead. Thanks for coming."

"Thanks for asking," Matt replied. He took a sip of the cider. It was definitely fruity, and the perfect refreshment for a warm summer night. "How has your day been? Is everything fixed up at The Seagull?"

"Yes, it's all back to normal. But let's not talk about that. All we ever seem to talk about is me and my problems. How was your day?"

"It was good. Quite low energy. I took a drive down the coast, stopped off for a look around Amble, then Newbiggin by the Sea. You're so lucky up here, having all these amazing towns so close by."

"That's true. Because I wasn't born here, I think I appreciate it more than those who've lived here all their lives. Lizzie thinks it's weird that I still get a buzz from walking along the beaches or wandering over to North Point. She grew up with the sea on her doorstep, so it's nothing special to her, but I love it."

Matt gazed out at the boats in the harbour. "You told me the other day you had your own boat. Which one is yours?"

Jake craned his neck. "You can't really see her from here. She's moored farther down the marina, away from the fishing boats." He pointed in the general direction. "I didn't think you were into boats."

"I'm not really. I just never met a boat owner before."

Jake laughed. "It's not as grand as it sounds. *The Golden Lady* accounts for every spare penny I have. It's not a cheap hobby. I think I told you this already, but she belonged to my stepdad, Jim. He bought her second-hand in the nineties, but she was built in the early eighties. I doubt she'd be worth much if I tried to sell her now, but I never would. She means too much to me. I know my way around boats and engines well enough to keep her in good working order myself. It's mainly the fuel and mooring that costs a fortune."

"Couldn't you make her pay? Maybe run trips along the coast to raise some extra income?"

"It's not worth it. The insurance alone is staggering. And I'd have to take time off from the café to run the trips, when The Seagull is a much stronger business prospect. I'm happy to keep boating as my very expensive hobby." He chuckled.

"You must show me sometime."

"I'd take you out on her, but I already know you don't have good sea legs. Maybe a little trip around the harbour, eh? As you can see, the water in here is as calm as a lake. And you know you'll be in safe hands."

"I don't doubt that. But I can get ill in a bathtub. I don't think your lifeboat training includes a cure for puking."

"Oh, you can do that over the side," he answered gamely. "Besides, *The Golden Lady* is a very stable old girl."

"Old girl?" he teased. "You realise your Golden Lady may be the same age as me, maybe even younger. I was made in the early eighties too."

"Well, when you see my boat, you'll realise she's in just as fine a condition as you are. They must have been doing something right in those days, eh?"

Matt threw back his head and laughed. "You're a sharp one. I'll give you that."

"Wait until you feel my teeth. You'll know when I take a bite."

Despite his youth, it was Jake who put Matt at ease. They finished their drinks and ordered two more. Jake was such easy company to be with — cheeky and flirtatious, with so much maturity and intelligence.

Matt knew plenty of men in their forties and fifties who lacked his wit and warmth. Several times as they sat there, people would call over and greet him with waves and good wishes.

"That's Minty. He's on the lifeboat crew with me," he said as one man waved across the terrace to him. Then later, "Oh, that's Angela. She runs the card shop on Portland Street." Jake seemed to be a popular and well-liked member of the Nyemouth community.

When they had finished their second drinks, they left the pub and headed for The Lobster Pot.

"I reserved the table for eight-thirty," Jake told him. "I thought we could have a drink first. They have a great cocktail bar at the front of the restaurant."

"It sounds like you're trying to get me drunk," Matt joked.

"Would that be a bad thing?"

"Ask again in an hour from now."

They were lucky enough to get another table outdoors. The terrace there was even busier than the pub. Situated farther along the marina, it caught the last of the sun, which had already left The Fisherman's Arms. Matt studied the cocktail menu.

"I think I'll have a Dark and Stormy," he said.

Jake wrinkled his face. "I'm not a fan of ginger ale. I think I'll have a Joe Collins."

"What's that?"

"It's like a Tom Collins but uses vodka in place of gin, with lemon juice and soda. It's quite refreshing."

After their cocktails arrived, Jake told him about life in the small seaside town, how bleak it could sometimes be in the winter.

"It's not all hardship," he explained. "They put an enormous Christmas tree up here in the harbour and lights all around. We always put on a big firework display for Guy Fawkes night in November and serve hot drinks and soup at the lifeboat station. It's usually a major fundraiser for us."

Jake's affection for the town came through in everything he said. His eyes twinkled and his face glowed with enthusiasm.

"Maybe I should come back in the autumn," Matt said. "I wonder if the house is available all year around."

"I should imagine so. Dominic moved in with Arnie earlier this year, and they're getting married soon. I don't think he has any plans to sell his old place, so I think he'll let it out long-term."

"Is that Arnie Walker, the actor? I read a bit about what happened here last summer."

"Yes. I missed all the action. Vince insisted we go on holiday to Mexico, so I was away at the time, though it was just as well. It was that awful holiday that convinced me to finally leave him. But the murder and rescue all happened when we were away. Arnie is a great guy, though you would never think he was a famous actor. He's so down-to-earth. And they make a lovely couple."

"It sounds like Nyemouth isn't as quiet and sleepy as people believe. There seems to be more going on here than back home in York."

"You probably don't know everything that happens in York. That's the real difference between cities and towns. Everyone is more aware of each other here. That can be both a good and a bad thing."

"You seem to have adjusted to it well. You fit right in, as though you'd lived here all your life."

"It seems that way at times. I actually wish I had. It would have been so cool to play at the beach as a kid."

"You came here when your mother remarried? What happened to her first husband?"

"He pissed off when I was a few months old. I have no idea where he is now. There are a few old photographs at home. He looked like I do, but I never think of him as Dad. He wasn't my father. Jim was." Jake sipped his drink and chuckled. "It goes some way to explaining my daddy issues, eh?"

"It sounds to me like you had a great mother and a fantastic step-family."

"I did. Everything worked out in the end. We seem to be talking about me again. How about you? Do you have a big family?"

"I'm the middle of three brothers," Matt said. "My dad stuck around until I was twelve and made just about every day a misery. He was nasty, violent and bad-tempered. The happiest day of my young life was when he left us. Everything was great for my mother and brothers after that. Apart from birthday and Christmas cards, I have had no contact with him in years."

"Wow, it sounds like we both bummed out in the father department. Is that why you went into the legal profession? To help families like your own?"

"Not consciously. At least, I don't think so, but it must have had an influence on the kind of law I ended up practicing. People make mistakes. They marry for the wrong reasons, but it doesn't mean they have to live with it forever. If I can get someone out of a bad situation, then I've done some good, especially if there are kids involved."

Jake suddenly looked very serious. "Thank God Vince was always too selfish to consider having children. He probably would have suggested it in time, if he thought it would have kept me with him longer, but I got out before we ever reached that stage."

"It happens."

Jake sipped his drink. "Let's not spoil the night talking about him. I came out because I wanted to get to know you better." He locked eyes with Matt as he spoke.

A delicious shiver ran all the way down Matt's spine. "Ask me anything you'd like. I'm an open book."

Jake winked. "I love a good book. And I'll enjoy getting stuck in this one."

Chapter Twelve

Jake wanted The Lobster Pot to impress Matt. Apart from his own café, it was his favourite place in town. When they'd first moved to Nyemouth, Jim had brought the family here for his mother's birthday, and it had become a tradition thereafter that they celebrated all major events at the venue. Vince, of course, had not been so hot on the place. He hated everything about Nyemouth and insisted that major celebrations should take place out of town. He preferred the bright lights and flashy restaurants of Newcastle. Jake had always felt out of place in the city that had once been his home and rarely enjoyed the overpriced food and drinks.

This was where his heart belonged.

Matt was making a good job of stealing his heart right now. Jake had warned himself not to get too involved, but sitting in one of the leather booths across from this hot guy, it was hard not to get carried away. The lighting was soft, with candles on the table, and Matt had never looked more gorgeous than he did right then.

Jake couldn't believe he was there. That a man like Matt, with his film-star good looks and successful legal career, would be interested in a small-town boy like him.

"You're just a cute, young twink," Vince had delighted in telling him. *"Most guys just want to fuck you for that. And your looks will fade with your youth. Soon, I'll be the only one who wants you."*

Though he'd discounted a lot of Vince's vile put-downs, that message had resonated. It had wormed into the foundation of his confidence and eroded it with time. Although they'd been flirting with each other all week and there was a tangible chemistry between them, the doubt remained. Matt was too good for Jake.

He tried to keep them at bay and enjoy the evening. It had been the best so far.

Kelly had greeted them with a knowing smile at the door and escorted them to the best booth at the rear of the restaurant. Its slight angle and high-backed seating gave them plenty of privacy, but its raised position allowed them to see out of the window to the darkening bay. As Matt studied the menu, Kelly gave Jake a raised thumb over his shoulder.

"Tell me what's good here," Matt had asked, and Jake was even more delighted to learn he had a love of seafood. Vince loathed it and would only ever order the fillet steak.

In the end, Matt had gone with Jake's recommendation of smoked trout with horseradish cream and salad for his starter. For their main course, he'd agreed to share the shellfish platter for two, which included a whole lobster, crab, langoustines, prawns, crayfish, oysters and mussels. He also ordered a bottle of Chablis, which was so delicious that they had finished it by the time they'd had their starters and ordered a second bottle to go with the main.

Jake felt lightheaded in the most wonderful way.

"This is amazing," Matt said, and popped one of the succulent langoustines in his mouth.

"It will all have come fresh off the boats this morning. Everything is fresh here. They don't use anything frozen. If it wasn't landed by the fishing fleet today or yesterday, it won't be on the menu. We get a lot of our own supplies from the fishermen here too, though we try not to compete with each other. The Seagull is a daytime café, so we don't get a lot of overlap in trade."

"I thought you all seemed very friendly, considering you're just a few doors away from each other."

"Nyemouth might be small, but there's room enough for both of us."

"It looks to me like you might be one of this place's best customers."

Jake chuckled. "Probably, though not as much as I'd like. Lizzie and I treat our staff to a night out here every couple of months. Thankfully, their taste doesn't run to lobster on those nights, but the simpler dishes are just as delicious."

When Jake excused himself to use the bathroom, Kelly intercepted him at the foot of the stairs.

"It looks like it's going well," she commented with a huge grin.

"Up to now it is."

"He looks really nice. Good manners too, unlike you-know-who."

"We're not talking about him tonight," Jake remarked.

"Good call," she laughed. "Listen… It's not like I'm spying on you or anything, but Lizzie texted earlier to ask how you were doing."

"That doesn't sound like spying at all," he said, taking it in good humour.

"Well, she texted again and told me to tell you not to worry about coming into the café at all tomorrow. She says have a good night and don't worry about a thing."

"I can't do that," he said, "but I appreciate the gesture. Let's see how the rest of the night goes, eh? Tell her I'll be there but won't commit myself to a time."

"That's what I like to hear," she said, coming in for a hug. "Enjoy the rest of your evening. You deserve it."

The main course had been cleared away when he returned to the table and Matt was studying the dessert menu.

"Got room for anything more?" he asked, looking up.

Jake shook his head. "Not another bite. But don't let me stop you if you want something."

Matt put down the menu. "It would be pure greed and nothing else if I did. To tell the truth, I don't have much of a sweet tooth. I've always preferred savoury food."

"Me too," Jake said, delighted they had something else in common. "I could usually go for a cheese plate after a meal, but I wouldn't have eaten so much for the main course if I wanted that. I'm perfectly satisfied."

"Oh, yeah?" Matt asked, raising a cheeky eyebrow.

"With the meal," he added, rising to the occasion. "But I could be tempted by dessert of a different kind."

Matt laughed. "I've never met anyone like you, you know that?"

"Oh. Is that a good thing?"

"When I was your age, I had none of your confidence. I was so quiet and serious all the way through university. And once I started working, I was all about my career."

"You seem laid-back now," Jake said.

"I am. But it took me a long time to get there. But you? You're amazing. You're funny, and you're brave. You've got a great business, lots of friends. You even own a boat. I mean, how cool is that?"

"I can picture you as a serious young man in your suit and a pair of nerdy glasses...like Clark Kent."

"Yeah, but you're the real-life superman, not me."

Jake blushed. He found compliments difficult to take, but he was flattered that Matt could think so much of him. Maybe he wasn't such a small-town nobody after all. Emboldened by the wine and Matt's comments, he leaned forward and asked, "What happens now? After this, I mean."

Matt leaned in too. His eyes appeared as deep as a twilight ocean in the light of the candles. "You mean when we leave here?"

Jake swallowed. "Yes."

"I'd love for you to come home with me."

Fantastic. "I'd love that too."

It had been on his mind all day—wondering where the evening would end. Would they enjoy a pleasant meal and go their separate ways? Or would they end up where he really wanted to be...in Matt's bed? He'd flipped back and forth, unsure of what would be the right thing to do. As badly as he wanted Matt, he knew it was the wrong time, with all the shit he had going down with Vince. But Matt was only here for another week. If they didn't take action now, there might never be another chance. He was torn, but throughout the day, his desire for Matt had seemed to outweigh every other consideration.

They asked for the bill. When it came, Matt took out his credit card.

"No," said Jake, pulling the silver tray across to his side of the table. "I invited you for the meal, so I'm going to pay for it."

Matt looked affronted. "You can't do that. I insist."

"Too bad, I'm paying for this."

"Let's split it, then. It's only fair."

Jake shook his head. "Don't argue. I asked you out, so I'm paying."

Matt surrendered. "All right, you win. But in that case, I want to take you out again, and next time I'll pay."

"I won't argue with that," Jake said, putting his card down on the tray. "I guess that means we're getting a second date."

"It definitely does."

It was dark when they left the restaurant around ten-thirty. The water in the harbour was low with the tide, lights reflecting on its still surface. Jake inhaled deeply, and as the fresh air hit him, he realised he was tipsy from the cocktails and the wine. *In a good way*, he noted. He wasn't drunk, just relaxed.

"Are you okay?" Matt asked, standing close to him. The scent of his aftershave was intoxicating.

Jake had an urge to grab him now and kiss him full on the mouth. Despite the alcohol reducing his inhibitions, he resisted. Nyemouth was a small town, and word would spread like wildfire if they saw him snogging a handsome stranger in the marina. And gossip like that would find its way to Vince in no time.

"I'm perfect," he replied. "Let's walk along the waterfront for a few minutes, just to blow the cobwebs away."

"Great idea."

Jake was taken by the romance of it all — of walking around the marina at night with an incredibly attractive man. All his boyhood ideals about adult relationships were captured in the moment. There had been no romance with Vince, not even at the start. Vince believed in grand, expensive gestures, like new cars, exotic holidays, buying designer clothes and watches, but he was never there in the present. His mind was always off elsewhere, thinking about his next big scheme or deal. He often laughed at the idea of going for a walk together or spending a day at the beach. There was never any time to appreciate what he had before him. *"How old are you? Five?"* Vince used to laugh at Jake's suggestion.

Jake had cherished every second of this evening, from the anticipation of meeting Matt to seeing him approach in The Fisherman's Arms. It was like he was taking part in a real-life movie. The kind of film he never wanted to end. A solid gold classic.

Finally, away from the nosey eyes of bars, he moved his hand towards Matt's and their fingers linked naturally. In the dark, Matt gave a soft gasp of appreciation.

"I'm ready now," Jake said. "Let's go to your place."

Chapter Thirteen

The nerves returned for Matt once they reached the house, when it was just the two of them alone in a small place. He tackled them in an instant. He wouldn't allow self-doubt or anxiety to spoil what had been a first-rate night so far. Jake wanted to be with him. The thought should make him want to climb the walls with joy.

Of course, Jake was so much younger than he was, and Matt already wondered what the younger man would make of his body. *Hell*, he thought, *might as well call it what it is – a middle-aged body.* Matt knew he was in good shape, better than a lot of his peers, but Jake was in the prime of his twenties. A man close to forty couldn't compare favourably with that.

If Jake had any reservations, they didn't show. He'd slipped his hand into Matt's down at the harbour and had left it there the whole way back. Despite his concerns, Matt hadn't stopped smiling since.

"I need to use the bathroom," Jake said, as Matt unlocked the door and turned on the lights. "That wine has gone right through me."

"Do you know where it is?"

"No. Upstairs, I guess."

"It's the first door at the top, straight across the hall."

Jake's absence gave him a few minutes to get himself together. Matt closed the curtains at the front windows and turned on two of the side lamps, creating a more intimate atmosphere. He went into the kitchen and poured a glass of water, drinking it straight off before refilling. He considered another shot of rum to take the edge off. *No, I've had more than enough alcohol tonight.* Instead, he opened the back door to allow some of the fresh sea air into the room.

He was sitting on the sofa in the living room when Jake returned. The light from one of the lamps was right behind Jake, and his silhouette revealed the powerful shape of his body—the wide, muscular shoulders, the swell of his biceps, the tight cinch of his waist...all of him perfection.

"Can I get you anything?" Matt asked, hating the awkwardness he felt, dreading that he would spoil the mood.

"Only this," Jake said.

Before Matt knew it was happening, Jake was on top of him, his thighs spread open across Matt's lap. He took Matt's head in both of his hands and fastened his mouth on top of his. Matt responded in an instant, sliding his hands around Jake's hips, letting them rest on the swell of his arse, and opened his mouth to take the younger man's tongue inside. His lips were delicious and soft, and the bristles of their stubble made a sexy sound as they rasped together.

Jake laughed softly and pressed his forehead against Matt's. "I've been wanting to do that since I saw you last Friday," he said. His breath was warm against Matt's face.

Matt gripped Jake's arse and pulled his hips against his body. He could not miss the hot hardness in Jake's trousers as it pressed against his belly. "And I've been dying to get my hands on this," he said, raising his lips for another kiss.

Jake murmured, grinding against Matt. He put his hands on Matt's shoulders and thrust his tongue into Matt's mouth.

Matt shuddered. The experience of being touched wasn't new. He hadn't been living a life of celibacy since leaving Clinton, but this experience was so unlike anything he'd known with those other men. His skin seemed to ripple beneath Jake's fingertips. As Jake grazed the skin of his neck, it caused a reaction all through his body.

"Let me see you," Matt whispered.

Jake straightened, still straddling Matt's lap. His cheeks were flushed with a delectable rosy glow, his mouth was open and he was breathing heavily. Jake unbuttoned his shirt from the neck down, moving his fingers with haste. Matt watched with wonder as the two halves dropped open, revealing his firm pecs and the dark brown curls that covered them. Jake shrugged the shirt from his shoulders and tossed it onto the floor. Matt went straight to his torso, unable to resist him.

He was perfect—a body teeming with youth and vigour, together with the fur and muscle of a mature man. The hair grew thick on his chest, thinning to a light trail down the centre of his body, then spread again across his abdomen. Hard nipples, small and pink, poked through the curls. Matt rubbed the pads of his thumbs over the tips, feeling them stiffen further.

There were no tattoos, no obvious scars or imperfections. He was flawless.

Matt held him by the waist again and sat up on the sofa, pressing his face against Jake's chest. The heat and scent of his body were intoxicating. He nuzzled his cheek against the soft hair, and Jake's heart beat strong and steadily against it.

Matt wanted more. He eased himself from the sofa, getting them both to their feet, before turning around and helping Jake into a sitting position.

"I want to see all of you," he said, drawing off Jake's left shoe, then the right, before going for his belt.

Jake followed his lead, leaning back onto the sofa. Matt unfastened his belt, then his fly. Jake raised his hips, allowing Matt to ease his chinos out from under his arse. Matt was overcome with impatience and grabbed Jake's underpants, hauling them down with his trousers. Jake's cock sprang free, slapping his belly. Matt pulled his trousers all the way down and Jake raised his legs to aid him.

Matt gasped at the sight of him naked, holding Jake behind the knees, keeping his thighs elevated and open. His cock was girthy and uncut. He had trimmed his pubes and shaved his balls. His nuts hung low, tantalising, half concealing his underside, where more glossy curls lined the route to his dark arse-crack.

"Oh my God," Matt gasped. "You're beautiful."

Jake let out an embarrassed laugh. "No," he said, "you are."

Those fat, heavy nuts were too much to resist. Matt bowed his head between Jake's thighs and drew his tongue along his scrotum. The skin was smooth and silky. Jake inhaled, and the sound was sharp through his teeth.

"Is that okay?" Matt asked, aware of the difference in their age and experience, fearful of overstepping the boundaries.

"It's amazing," Jake assured him. "I'm not used to it, that's all. Keep going. I love it."

Encouraged, Matt went back down. He took his time, giving Jake's testicles lots of attention. He licked each one in turn, ever so gently, feeling the weight of them on his tongue. Without a doubt, Jake had the biggest balls of any man he'd ever been with. He rose higher, bathing the thick root of his cock in saliva, before tracking the veins along the underside to the tip. Jake's foreskin covered his penis all the way to the end. Matt probed with the tip of his tongue, tasting the saltiness of his sticky pre-cum. He gripped the shaft, tilting it towards him, before taking it into his mouth.

"Oh my God," Jake exclaimed in a rush, his knees jerking.

Matt froze, looking into his eyes for assurance.

"It's okay," Jake groaned. "It's…uh, just keep going."

Matt obliged, taking him all the way to the back of his throat. It was obvious from his reactions that Vince had paid little attention to his husband. The man was an even bigger idiot than Matt had previously thought. Only a fool would neglect this gorgeous young man.

Jake pushed his fingers into Matt's hair. His touch was light. He didn't try to control Matt in any way, just heightened the connection between them. The head of his cock nudged the back of Matt's throat. It was a stretch to take him all the way. Despite the ache in his jaw, Matt rose to the challenge. He bowed his head back and forth, very gently, keeping him deep.

"Stop," Jake said. "Whoa, whoa, whoa."

Matt eased back, still holding him at the root. "Are you all right?"

"I'm perfect," Jake said, his chest heaving. "I just don't want to come yet. A few more seconds of that and I'd have been gone."

Matt grinned, going back to work on his balls, rolling them around on his tongue.

"This isn't fair," Jake protested with a cocky grin. "Why am I bare-arse naked and you're still fully dressed?"

"Good point." Matt got to his feet and held out his hand, helping Jake off the sofa. "Let's go upstairs so we can do this properly."

Jake flung his arms around Matt's neck and pressed his hot, naked body tight against him. As they kissed, Matt couldn't resist going for a feel of his butt, taking the cheeks in both hands, squeezing the firm flesh. Jake ground his hips, pushing his arse against Matt's palms.

"Are we going to go all the way?" Jake whispered, their lips close together.

"If that's what you want," Matt replied, kissing the side of his mouth.

"You might not have noticed, but I'm gagging for it."

They both laughed. Matt gave his butt a playful slap. "Then let's go upstairs."

Matt slipped his hand around Jake's bare waist and took him to the bedroom. There was something intensely erotic about being fully clothed beside this beautiful naked man. As they went up the stairs, Matt positioned Jake in front of him so he could admire his peachy arse as he took each step. His cheeks were lightly furred, with the hair growing darker and thicker around the crack. Matt couldn't wait to get stuck in here. He wasn't a fan of the modern trend for young guys to wax and shave every part of their bodies. A little grooming was essential, but he preferred men who left some of what nature intended rather than doing away with the whole lot. He enjoyed the slight jiggle and bounce of Jake's arse as he walked ahead of him.

Had he ever met a guy who turned him on as much as this? Not even in his late teens or early twenties, when every man he met got him horny... Jake was hotter than anyone.

At the top of the stairs, he put his hand around Jake's waist and guided him to the bedroom. He turned on the bedside lamp, keeping the ambience low and warming. Jake's body was a fantasy made flesh in the soft light. His beautiful cock leaned out in front of him.

"Now for your part of the deal," Jake said. "Strip."

Matt kicked off his shoes. He took his time, not because he was self-conscious of his body, but because he wanted this to be special—a moment they would both remember. He watched Jake as he undressed, seeing the way his eyes widened when Matt discarded his shirt. Matt wasn't vain about his looks and did enough exercise to know he was in good shape. His body might not be perfect, like Jake's, but he felt confident enough. Unlike Jake, his chest and torso was smooth. Save for a small treasure trail below his navel.

He unfastened his belt and trousers and shoved them to his feet before stepping out of them. In a pair of dark trunks, his arousal was unmistakable, leaning along his left hip. Having seen Jake's cock already, Matt knew they were well matched in endowment. The major difference between them was that Jake had a foreskin while he was circumcised. He skidded his trunks to his ankles and kicked them away. *The final reveal.*

Jake licked his lips. "Wow. You're so hot."

Matt took two long strides, closing the distance between them, and wrapped his arms around Jake's torso, pulling him close for maximum skin-on-skin contact. They ground their hips together, squeezing their cocks in the tightness between. Jake wandered his hands to Matt's arse, and Matt groaned from deep in his chest as he squeezed and caressed his cheeks. Jake could do anything he wanted, take whatever he wanted from him. Matt would go along with every one of his desires.

"What would you like?" he whispered along Jake's neck and gently nipped the flesh with his teeth.

Jake shuddered. Matt quickly came to realise how sensitive he was.

"I want you to fuck me," Jake said, throwing back his head to expose his throat.

"You're sure?" Matt moved his lips across his collar bone.

"I've wanted you inside me since I first saw you. I've never been surer of anything."

Matt grinned. "Then let's get you ready."

He guided Jake to the bed, laying him on his back before hauling his hips to the edge. Matt dropped to his knees. Jake knew what he was doing. He grabbed the backs of his knees, raising and widened his legs. Matt took a moment to appreciate the view, the double curve of his cheeks, his heavy balls hanging halfway down to his exposed arsehole. Though naturally hairy, Jake had clipped the hair in his crack, keeping it clear and clean. Matt scooted forward and ran his tongue along the honey-brown creases of his opening.

"Oh, fuck," Jake jerked upon the bed.

"Are you okay?" Matt asked. "Don't you like it?"

He exhaled, blowing out his cheeks. "I love it. I'm not used to it, that's all. Vince would never do that to me."

"Let me guess... He had no problem with you going down on him."

"Got it in one," Jake said.

"Then let me show you what you've been missing."

He slithered his tongue slowly along the lines, circling the opening, taking his time, making sure Jake would enjoy every second. The way his thighs trembled and his breath came in ragged gasps told Matt he was doing everything right. With expert dedication, he coaxed Jake's hole into slippery submission.

"I think you're ready," he said at last. Though he could have eaten that delicious young arse for hours, he was keen to give Jake what he wanted—what they both wanted—and get inside him. "Give me a few seconds."

Matt retrieved a condom and a sachet of lube from his toiletry bag in the en suite bathroom. Jake maintained his position, his butt at the edge of the bed, hands hooked around his knees, holding his legs open, exposing that sweet, glistening hole. Matt opened the condom and put it on with care, rolling the rubber all the way down his meaty shaft. He squeezed lube into his fist and pumped it over his dick, getting a good coating, before smearing it around Jake's opening, easing his finger inside to prepare the deeper passage. Jake's feet twitched and Matt sought his assurance before going further.

"I'm fine," Jake said, his cheeks flushed. "Out of practise, that's all. Don't stop. I want you inside me."

Matt worked his finger in all the way to the knuckle, getting plenty of the lube inside. He pushed and pulled with a rotating motion. The tight route began to ease and soften around him. Satisfied, he withdrew his finger and stepped up close to the bed. He dipped his knees to get the angle right, positioning himself, and pushed. He took it slowly, easing into the tight passage no more than a couple of centimetres.

"It's that all right for you?" he asked.

Jake nodded, his face rosy, his eyes wide with innocent desire. "Keep going."

Matt obliged, leaning into Jake until the whole head of his cock was inside. "Tell me if it hurts you," he said.

"Don't worry. I will."

He took Jake's ankles and lifted them onto his shoulders, then stepped right up to the bed to slide the rest of the way in. Somewhere inside Jake, a resistance gave, and he glided in until his hips and balls pressed against Jake's upturned butt. He waited, giving his young lover time to adjust.

"How is that?" he asked, stroking the outside of Jake's thighs.

"Feels big," he answered. In the soft lamp light, Matt noticed the sweat beads glistening on his brow.

"You're gorgeous," Matt said, turning his head to kiss the inner skin of Jake's ankle.

His hole, feverishly hot and snug, was pure paradise. When he felt certain Jake was ready, Matt fucked him slowly, wanting it to last, wanting to give Jake all the pleasure his husband had denied him. Jake sighed and threw his hands above his head, exposing his manscaped armpits, surrendering entirely to Matt.

Matt slid his hands beneath Jake's butt, raising his arse slightly off the bed to increase the angle that would bring his cock in direct contact with Jake's prostate. Jake's eyes widened in surprise with Matt's next forward stroke. Matt grinned. He had hit the target.

Jake's mouth opened in a silent question.

"Feels good, doesn't it?" Matt said, going at him with a long stroke.

"What? Whoa, what are you doing?"

"Just enjoy it," he whispered, loving every second of fucking this exceptional man.

"Oh…my…God…," Jake dragged out, arching his back from the bed. "What is that?"

"You'll see," Matt murmured, maintaining the steady rhythm. Controlling his own passion was easy. He was so focused on giving Jake everything he deserved.

Jake shot his head up from the bed, staring at Matt with wide surprise. "Oh, God, I'm gonna come."

His hands were nowhere near his cock when the first blast of white cum flew into the air. It arched clean over his chest and belly to splat on his shoulder and the bed beyond. The second spurt was even bigger, an eruption that covered the curly hair on his pecs in sticky ribbons. The spasms caused his arse to tighten. Matt increased his thrusts, knowing he was close. While Jake's cock continued spewing its milky load all over his belly, Matt rolled over the edge, roaring through clenched teeth as he ejaculated deep inside the condom in Jake's exquisite hole. His knees trembled, and he gripped Jake's arse in both hands just to stay upright.

They both drew in great, gasping breaths of air when they were done.

"*What* was that?" Jake cried, his face split by the biggest smile.

"I guess you haven't experienced that before. That was your prostate." Matt withdrew, keeping hold of the condom, and eased Jake's ankles from his shoulders.

"I've heard it could do that, but I always figured it was a myth," he said, still catching his breath. "I didn't think it really made that much difference."

He's obviously never been with a man who knows what he's doing, Matt thought, but said nothing. He didn't want to bring up the subject of Vince after such an incredible experience.

Jake rolled off the edge of the bed. "I'll just clean up," he said, going down the hall to the main bathroom. Matt figured he wanted a moment of privacy and disposed of the condom in the en suite. He checked his reflection in the mirror and saw that his face, neck and shoulders were flushed.

"Take it easy, old man, or you'll give yourself a heart attack," he told himself.

He hoped Jake wouldn't want to leave straight afterwards. A lot of guys often did the minute sex was over, but he hoped they had something more meaningful than that. What he really wanted was for Jake to stay the night. He flopped naked on top of the bed, hoping Jake would take the hint when he returned.

It would be so easy to develop deep feelings for Jake.

You already have feelings for him — and strong ones at that.

Not because of the sex. Matt had fallen for him more deeply each time they'd met. There was something special between them, something difficult to define.

Jake came back into the bedroom. Matt was glad to see him still naked. He hadn't snuck downstairs to collect his clothes, ready for a hasty exit. He climbed straight onto the bed and snuggled in against Matt. Matt put his arm around his shoulder.

"Feeling good?"

"The best." Jake pressed a kiss against Matt's chest. "Not one word of a lie, I have never been fucked like that before. What you just did? My God, that was intense."

"I loved it too," Matt said. "I'm happy we both did."

"I'm still a little shaken. My legs were wobbling when I came back along the hall."

"Keep the compliments coming. You don't know how much they mean to an old fart like me."

"You're not old. Stop putting yourself down. There's, what, like twelve years between us?"

"Almost fourteen," Matt corrected.

"Big deal… That's nothing. And I don't know any younger men who could do what you just did to me. I didn't even touch myself and you made me come. That's never happened before."

Matt ruffled his hair. "It doesn't happen every time. Don't get used to it. It could just have been because you weren't used to it."

Jake stretched and rubbed the entire length of his body against Matt. "Well, there's only one way to find out, and that's doing it again."

Matt laughed. "And that proves the real age difference between us. You might have the stamina to go again already, but I'm gonna need quite some time to recharge these batteries."

"How about in the morning?"

"So, you're staying?"

"If it's all right with you."

"I hoped you would."

Matt hugged him tighter. No one knew what the next few days would bring, but for tonight, at least, they were together. He would sleep better because of it.

Chapter Fourteen

Jake rolled against the naked body in bed beside him and pressed his chest and belly into the curve of Matt's back. Despite having slept very little during the night, his head was clear and he felt wonderfully refreshed this morning. Resting his head on the pillow behind Matt, he inhaled the warm, sleepy scent of his hair.

Jake could not get enough of him. He couldn't resist touching him, reaching out for him, assuring himself he was still there, luxuriating in the heat and hardness of his body, needing to feel the connection of bare skin against skin. They had made love three times since coming to bed, and Jake would happily take more.

He raised his head to check the time. Almost seven-thirty. He'd texted Lizzie when he went to the bathroom earlier to let her know he'd take up her offer for a late start today. He had no intention of taking the whole day off, but the prospect of another hour or two in bed with Matt was too much of a temptation to resist.

Jake swept his hand along the curve of Matt's naked waist. He had an amazing body. All that walking and hiking kept him in terrific shape. Jake had noted the thick muscle of his thighs and calves as he'd manoeuvred him around the bedroom and the beefy chunks of his buttocks when he'd gone to get rid of the condoms. Everything he found attractive in a man, Matt had it all going on. And stamina, too. Jake smiled as he remembered being fucked every which way across this bed. Matt hadn't flagged once.

And all the things he'd done to Jake... The riming, his kissing, the expert way he'd pounded his prostate into the most mind-blowing orgasms.

Jake had experienced none of that before. Vince had been very unadventurous in bed. He liked Matt to lie face down while he'd jabbed at his arse from behind. It rarely took Vince long to come, and there was no such thing as foreplay unless he'd wanted Jake to go down on him. He was never keen to reciprocate a blow job, and there was no way he'd ever put his lips near Jake's arse. Matt had got stuck into all those things and seemed to do it with relish.

Jake moved his hand to fondle Matt's behind, stroking the smooth flesh beneath the covers. He wondered whether Matt liked to get fucked too — or whether he was one of those older guys who refused to entertain the idea. It seemed unlikely, when he was so open and exciting in other ways. Jake had been happy to let Matt fuck him senseless, and he'd enjoyed every second of it but was keen to explore Matt's body in every way he could. Maybe they could try it sometime. He'd love to get stuck into such a hot piece of arse.

He gave Matt's ripe flesh an appreciative squeeze.

"You're insatiable," Matt muttered into the pillow.

"Sorry. Did I wake you?"

"You did. But it's a lovely way to start the day."

Jake shuffled closer, putting his arm around Matt and spooning in behind him. His hard cock slipped naturally into the cleft of his bottom. Matt gave a little laugh and pushed his hips back against Jake's sticky penis.

This is a dream come true, Jake thought. Waking up beside this hot guy, having him respond in all the right ways when Jake touched him, not pulling away or rushing to get Jake out of the house. He had no idea where things would go from there, but for a first night together, it couldn't have gone better.

"Did you sleep well?" he asked.

"When I got the chance," Matt replied, turning his head in Jake's direction. "You sure know how to put a man through his paces."

"I didn't see you having any trouble keeping up."

"And I'm more surprised by that than anyone. You're incredible, you know that?"

"I think you are," Jake snuggled in tighter. "This is lovely."

"Mm-m, it sure is."

At any other time, Jake would have felt guilty about not getting to work. Friday mornings were busier than others. It was the day when office and shop workers treated themselves to a takeaway breakfast or a speciality coffee on their way to work. The Seagull would already be doing good business.

It could wait.

Not even his loyalty to Lizzie and the café could pull him out of this sweet embrace.

"What are your plans for today?" he asked, nuzzling the back of Matt's neck.

"Hmm-m, nothing major. I might go for a drive south if the weather stays nice. I've been meaning to take a look around Tynemouth. A bit of a wander, a spot of lunch... That's the extent of my ambitions for today."

"Sounds like a nice idea."

"Why don't you come with me?"

"It's tempting, but I really do have to go to work. I know Lizzie tried to cut me some slack, but it wouldn't be fair to leave it all to her. We didn't pull in any extra help like we would if I were taking a proper day off, so she'll have most of the cooking to do."

Matt rolled over onto his back, looking at Jake sideways.

Jesus, how can anyone look that sexy first thing in the morning?

His thick hair was mussed, but it suited him perfectly. And from the glint in his eyes, no one would know he'd had a night of crazy sex and minimal sleep.

"Got time for some breakfast before you go?" Matt asked.

"That depends what you have in mind," Jake said, snaking his hand to Matt's groin and delighted to find him already hard.

"I'm worried that thing will fall off if we're not careful. It hasn't had so much action in the space of twelve hours since...well, ever."

"How about if I promise to go very easy on you?"

Matt grinned, leaning over for a kiss. "I think that could work."

Jake raised the covers to straddle Matt's waist. This was going to make him even later for work, but right at that moment, he didn't care. This wonderful man beneath him was all that mattered.

* * * *

Saw Jake out with a guy at The Lobster Pot last night. Are you two finally moving on?

Vince Ashfield read the text three times and his fist tightened around the phone. The message had come from Ian Marlow, a fellow wholesale operator and occasional business partner. Ian lived on the outskirts of Morpeth but regularly took his clients to The Lobster Pot when he wanted to wine and dine them.

Vince had never understood why. There were far more impressive places in Newcastle. When he wanted to make an impact on his potential customers, Vince would take them there, not some two-bit small-town shithole. For some reason, Jake had always been a fan of that stinking fish restaurant too.

Vince, sitting in his high-backed leather chair in his office overlooking the general warehouse below, ground his teeth. He knew what Ian was going to tell him. He'd had suspicions all week about what Jake was up to, but he hit the dial icon to call him up anyway.

"Who was he out with?" he asked, skipping the small talk.

"Hello to you too," Ian said. His glee was clear in his voice, and Vince didn't have to see him to know the smirking expression he'd have written all over his face. "From your hasty reply, I take it you're not too happy with this development."

"Who was it?" Vince kept the anger out of his tone.

"I didn't recognise the fella," Ian replied. "They looked like they were pretty cosy though. So, are you seeing other people now?"

How to answer that? Vince didn't want word getting around that Jake was making a fool of him, and Ian was a gobshite. He would spread the news around everyone he contacted today.

"Jake is going through a rebellious phase, that's all. He'll get it out of his system soon enough."

"I don't know why you bother. If he doesn't appreciate the lifestyle you've given him, cut him loose — the ungrateful little shit."

Vince grimaced. Ian, three-times divorced, traded in girlfriends every six months or so. The last girl Vince had seen him with had looked like she was still at school. It had been hard to tell under the make-up and false eyelashes. Ian liked them young, unpolished and very obliging. Vince wasn't about to take relationship advice from him.

"What did this man look like?" he asked. "I just want to know who he is."

"I dunno. He was a bloke. I didn't pay much attention. Dark hair, late-thirties maybe. Good-looking, I'd say, if I were the type of bloke to notice those things. It looked like they were well into each other, giving it googly eyes across the table. You're better off without him if he's out there making a mug of you with other fellas."

"Thanks, Ian. I appreciate the notice."

"I can hook you up, if you're looking to get back at him. Charmaine's little brother is gay. Cute young thing too. He's just the type you want on your arm. That would make Jake jealous all right, seeing you with a younger model." Ian gave a dirty laugh.

"There's no need. Thanks for your message." Vince hung up.

The cheating little bastard. The no-good fucking whore. Parading around the town with that smug cunt he picked up last weekend.

Vince smashed his fist on the desk.

He'd known without a doubt that Jake was up to something. Vince didn't get to where he was today — the boss of a major international wholesale business — without trusting his instincts. He'd had a feeling all along that there was more to the incident up on South Bank Terrace last week than had appeared. Jake had probably been there to hook up with the guy in Dominic Melton's old place when Vince had tracked him down. *The guileful skank.*

A knock at the door interrupted Vince's seething. Pete, a young apprentice at the warehouse, came in with his morning coffee. Vince insisted that they brought him a large latte made with full-fat milk and a chocolate biscuit at eleven each day. Pete was learning the admin routine from his secretary Denise, and one of the first jobs he'd learned on day one was how to make the boss' favourite drink.

"Your coffee, Mr Ashfield," the young man said, backing through the door with the latte glass and saucer, and a chunky biscuit on a separate plate.

Vince was about to bark some irate comment at the kid, but held his tongue. It wasn't Pete's fault Vince had married the town tramp.

For the first time, Vince paid attention to the young apprentice, noticing the snug fit of his cheap grey trousers across his pert butt cheeks. Once through the door, Pete straightened up and came over to his desk.

Not a bad looking boy, Vince thought. He still had some growing to do and the remnants of adolescent acne blemished his face, but he was filling out in all the right places. He had a decent set of shoulders on him and small pecs that bulged through his slim-fitting shirt. There was too much product in his dark blond hair, but he had bright green eyes that were rather dazzling. He reminded Vince of Jake when they'd first met—typical Nyemouth trash, but not without potential.

"How are you doing, Pete?"

The boy looked startled by the question. Vince barely looked up when he brought the coffee in most days.

"F-fine, Mr Ashfield."

"How long have you been working here now?" Vince asked.

"Coming up to six months," Pete replied.

As long as that? Vince really hadn't been paying attention. Or maybe he had blossomed in that time. He was still at that age when the body and face were changing all the time. "How old are you?"

Now the boy looked nervous. "Nineteen, sir."

The same as Jake when Vince had picked him out of the gutter. Maybe there was something in what Ian had said about making Jake jealous with a younger model. This boy could be the one to do it. With a decent haircut, some good clothes, a quality face wash to clear away the rest of that acne... *Yes*, he thought, *not a bad idea at all.* He'd show Jake what he was missing and how easy it was for him to fuck around too.

"Do you have a girlfriend?" Vince asked, looking directly into his eyes.

The boy couldn't maintain the contact. He stared at the desk, his face turning a deepening shade of scarlet. "No, sir."

"Very wise. You don't want to get yourself tied down with some silly girl—not a man in the prime of his life like you are." Vince's gaze drifted to his groin. Pete's trousers were so tight he didn't have to use much imagination to guess what delights they contained. Some of these dumb town-boys were hung like horses. Pete looked like he'd be no exception.

Vince resolved to keep an eye on Pete. He could be just the pick-me-up he needed.

"You can get back to work now," he said, noticing the relief on Pete's face. He found that kind of innocence quite endearing. It would be so much fun to corrupt him.

Alone again, his thoughts returned to Jake and his anger level quickly rose. It would not be enough to make him jealous, not if he was swanning around with this fancy new bloke. Vince would have to teach him a real lesson.

It was obvious now that smashing up the café had not been enough.

He had to think bigger than that.

Vince picked up his phone and hit the intercom switch. "Moody and Curtis to the main office," he said, repeating it to be sure they heard.

Moody and Curtis were the most useful and dedicated members of his crew — hardworking in the warehouse, but always on the lookout for ways to earn extra cash. Moody had taken care of the windows at The Seagull for a twenty-pound note in his back pocket and case of cheap beer.

Vince would offer the pair a lot more for the task he now had in mind.

Chapter Fifteen

Jake hadn't intended to see Matt again so soon, but when he sent a text in the late afternoon to say he'd picked up some fresh seafood on his travels and would Jake like to join him for dinner at home that evening, it was an offer he could not resist. At six-thirty on Friday evening, he walked up the steep path to South Bank Terrace with a bag loaded with clinking bottles he'd picked up at the grocery store on his way. It was a balmy night, and he'd dressed casually in shorts and a linen shirt.

The truth was, though, that while he'd tried to play it cool with himself, he'd been unable to think about anything other than Matt all day. Lizzie and most of their staff had commented on the dopey grin he'd worn while moving about the kitchen. When he'd left Matt after breakfast, they'd made vague plans to catch up again over the weekend, but Jake had regretted the cool attitude as soon as he'd left. He'd been wondering about how soon he should leave it before texting Matt, when the invitation to dinner had come through.

Perfect timing.

Matt greeted him at the door as soon as he opened the garden gate.

"I saw you coming," Matt said breezily. He was barefoot, looking casually chic in a short-sleeved white shirt and thigh length chino shorts. An unruly lock of dark hair hung over his brow. Jake recognised the look. Working in a hot kitchen quickly dishevelled the smartest hair style.

They shared a warm, inviting kiss at the door before Jake stepped inside.

Breezy pop music played from a speaker in the corner of the kitchen. Matt had his ingredients already prepared on chopping boards. The doors to the patio were open, allowing a waft of fresh air into the hot interior.

Jake handed over the bag of wine. "It all came out of the chiller, so it should still be cool."

"Perfect," Matt said, putting all but one of the bottles in the fridge and grabbing two glasses from the cupboard. "Let's take this outside."

Jake couldn't resist checking out his butt as he followed Matt onto the patio. Those shorts did wonders for his high and juicy peach. Matt flopped onto the sofa and curled a tanned leg beneath him. He set the glasses on the table and poured the wine.

"Chardonnay," he commented on the label. "Excellent choice."

"You said you were cooking seafood. I didn't think I could go wrong with Chardonnay."

"I hope your expectations aren't too high. This won't compare to the meal we had last night. I had to talk to Jacob next door for advice on how to cook some of the stuff I'd bought. I felt adventurous when I saw the fresh fish shop in Amble, but my enthusiasm exceeds my cookery skills."

"Fresh sea food doesn't need a lot of fancy cooking. The simpler the recipe, the better."

"That's exactly what Jacob said. I still got him to write his instructions down, though."

Jake laughed. It was sweet to see that Matt had made so much of an effort.

There was a hardback book on the table. Jake picked it up. It was an old copy of *Jaws* by Peter Benchley.

"Is this what you're reading?" he asked.

"Yeah. I picked it up at the shop in town."

"No wonder you don't like going out in boats. I don't think reading this will help."

Matt grinned. "It makes a great summer read, especially when I can hear the sea while I'm reading it."

They drank a glass of wine and Matt filled him in on his day, the places he'd visited on his tour of the south coast of Northumberland. His eyes twinkled as he described the towns and villages he'd stopped at, and it was obvious he'd become as smitten with the area as Jake had himself when his mother had first moved them here. It was too soon for him to hope that Matt might want to make deeper ties with the Northeast. This was nothing more than a holiday fling for him. To expect anything more would only lead Jake to despair.

He couldn't allow himself to go there.

"What time do you want to eat?" Matt asked at last.

"I'm not really hungry yet, but whenever you're ready is good for me."

"I'm not hungry either. I had a good lunch this afternoon."

"So, what are you cooking tonight? Or is that a surprise?"

"Well, I love Italian food, and as Jacob told me to keep it simple, I'm doing seafood linguine. I've got a mix of prawns, mussels and cod. I'll cook them in a light sauce of olive oil, wine, garlic and parsley."

"That sounds delicious. I love Italian food too. We don't have a restaurant here in town, but there are some great Italian places nearby. You should check them out before you leave."

"Is that another date?" Matt asked.

"It is if you want it to be."

He licked his bottom lip. "I definitely want it to be."

"Then it's a date. Let's do it one night next week."

The idea of going out with Matt again made him giddy. Suddenly Jake jumped out of his seat and threw himself on top of Matt, straddling his lap to take him in a deep, open-mouthed kiss. Matt responded, pushing his tongue against Jake's and cupping his palms around his arse. Jake ground his hardness against Matt's belly, showing him the extent of his arousal. Seconds later, they tore at each other's clothes.

Their shirts came off first and Jake pressed his chest against Matt's, revelling in the heated contact of his skin. He inhaled the sexy, warm scent of his body and hair.

Jake looked quickly around, checking that the windows of Jacob's house next door didn't look down on them.

"This patio is private, right?" he asked, his lips open against Matt's.

"As far as I can tell. There's no way for anyone to see in."

That was all Jake needed to hear. He tore at Matt's belt. They rolled onto their sides on the wide outdoor sofa, fumbling and kissing. Jake shoved Matt's shorts and underwear to mid-thigh, getting a handful of his lush bare butt. As Matt tore Jake's shorts down, their cocks rubbed together, hot, hard and wet.

Jake rolled on top of Matt and kicked his shorts all the way off. He rose onto his knees and wrapped his hand around Matt's throbbing dick, squeezing, tugging.

"Is this okay?" he asked, unused to handling a circumcised penis.

"Uh-huh," Matt nodded, taking Jake's cock in a similar grip.

Fast and furious, they brought each other to shuddering relief, spraying a hot double load over Matt's chest and abdomen.

Jake sat back on his knees, catching his breath, laughing, holding up his right hand to show the cum running down the backs of his knuckles. "That was something else," he gasped.

"I haven't prepared a starter," Matt said, looking up at him rosy-faced. "I guess that will have to do instead."

They both roared.

This was a whole new experience for Jake. A sexual partner who could make him laugh as hard as he came. *I can get used to this.*

* * * *

To Matt's great relief, Jake offered to shell and devein the prawns he had bought. Even after Jacob's careful instructions, he still wasn't sure where to start with them.

"I feel bad," he said. "I invited you to dinner and now you have to pitch in."

"Think of me as your sous chef. I'm helping with the prep, but you still have to do all the cooking yourself."

"That sounds like a fair deal."

They had cleaned up after their alfresco quickie and were ready to eat. It amazed Matt how easy he found it to have Jake around. They seemed to fit together so well as they navigated the small kitchen space. Jake topped up their wine glasses before taking a seat at the table with two bowls and set about shelling the prawns, while Matt put a large pan of salted water on to boil for the pasta and began to sweat the garlic down in lots of extra virgin olive oil.

He was playing a random list of music on his phone, all summer pop tunes, and a great old track from Kylie Minogue came on. "I love this one," he said, gently swaying to the music as he moved about the kitchen in bare feet.

"Me too," Jake said. "It was one of my mam's favourites."

Matt nodded, but the comment immediately got him thinking about the difference in their ages. Thirteen years wasn't so great, he had to remind himself. It wasn't as if he could be Jake's dad, not unless he'd started really young. He had to get over the age thing. It didn't seem to bother Jake at all. He was the one who would take the heat from his friends for dating an old man. If Jake was fine with it, why should he be so hung up?

Jake brought the shelled prawns over to the counter. He brushed against Matt as he passed. Matt stirred, leaning back against his chest a little. *This sure feels nice.*

"Are we eating in here?" Jake asked, nuzzling the back of his neck. "I'll set the table."

"It's a pleasant night. Why not lay the stuff outside? There's some tea lights already out there. You could light those."

"Sounds like a plan." Jake planted a kissed on his cheek before getting on with the job.

Matt couldn't help smiling as he added the linguine to the pan of water. Things had never been this easy with Clinton, not even at the start of their relationship. Clinton had done nothing to help around the house, and the romance of eating outside by candlelight would have been lost on him. He had to be where the action was—in the bars, clubs and casinos. A quiet night in just wasn't his style.

Though he'd only known Jake a week, things were so different between them, so comfortable.

Is that good or bad? he wondered. Neither he nor Jake were really in a position to judge, going off their previous relationship failures. It felt good. He couldn't deny that. Maybe that was enough for now, and he shouldn't push or question it further.

As the pasta cooked, he sliced the baguette he'd bought at a bakery that afternoon and took it out to the patio where Jake had set the table, lit the candles and put out another bottle of wine in a cooler. Matt's heart bounded in his chest at the sight, and he caught his breath. He wouldn't have believed one week ago that it would be possible to have such a perfect evening. He'd come on holiday expecting to be alone most of the time. He had not expected this.

It took no more than a few minutes to finish the pasta and cook the seafood to Jacob's instructions.

"Wow," Jake said, as he carried two bowls to the table. "That smells incredible. I don't think I believe you when you say you haven't cooked this before."

"Wait until you've tried it before passing judgement," he said, taking the chair across from Jake.

"If it tastes half as good as it smells, it's going to be wonderful."

Jake's golden skin glowed in the light of the candles. Once again, Matt couldn't believe his luck at getting to spend time with this exceptional young man.

The food was indeed good. Matt didn't know his way around seafood and shellfish as much as Jake, but it tasted really special to him. Jake assured him it was outstanding.

"If you ever feel like a change of career, I can put a good word in for you at The Lobster Pot. This would fit right in on their menu."

Matt laughed out loud. "That's a hell of a compliment, but I think you might be a little biased."

"Me? No way. I'm a professional cook myself, remember. I know what I'm talking about. If this is your first attempt, imagine how great you could be with practice."

"I'll take the compliment, but I think it's mainly due to the quality of the ingredients. I could never replicate this with the stuff I can buy from the supermarket back in York. Trust me."

"I know. If I have to buy from supermarkets, I usually choose from the freezer rather than the fresh counter. They freeze most of the stuff fresh after catching, but a lot of the supposedly fresh seafood can be a week old, if not more."

Matt found Jake even more fascinating the longer he spent time with him. His interests and depth of knowledge were vast. He'd heard Jake refer to himself as a small-town boy several times, as though that were a bad thing, but there was nothing small about his way of thinking. Though Matt didn't want to think about Clinton, it was hard not to compare the two of them. For two nights running, he'd enjoyed wonderful conversations over dinner with Jake, where in the years he was Clinton, their evening meals had always been accompanied by the soundtrack of early evening soap operas.

Jake cleared his bowl and mopped up the last of the sauce with chunks of bread.

"Delicious," he said as he wiped the bowl clean.

"I've been thinking," Matt said, twirling his wine glass by the stem.

"What about?"

"Your boat."

"Oh."

"What's it called again, *The Golden Lady*?"

Jake nodded enthusiastically. "Do you still want to take a look around her? I'm only working half a day on Monday, if you want to see her."

"I want to do more than that," he said. "Does your offer of a ride along the coast still stand?"

Jake's eyes widened. "Of course. I thought you didn't want to."

"I didn't," he admitted. "But I've changed my mind. I'm kind of nervous about going out to sea, but I can't think of anyone more experienced or knowledgeable to do it with. If you still want to, I'd love to come out on your boat."

"Okay. Well, the weather forecast for Monday looks pretty good at the minute. If it holds up over the weekend, we could go for a little run up north. I wouldn't take you out unless the conditions were absolutely calm. The old lady can roll a little in a swell, but if the weather is good, we could cruise a little, find a nice bay to drop the anchor and go ashore for a picnic. How does that sound?"

"Amazing."

"And don't worry," he said cheekily. "There's nothing like *Jaws* in the seas off here."

After the meal, they had coffee outside before going up to the bedroom to make love again, slowly. At a little after eleven, Jake reached for his clothes and started to dress.

"I wish you could stay," Matt said, watching him from the bed.

"I do too, but I'm on early at the café. I can't let Lizzie down two mornings in a row."

He nodded. "Of course. Will I see you tomorrow?"

"Again, I'd love to, but I've already got plans. One of the guys from the crew is getting married in a couple of weeks. Tomorrow night is his stag party."

Matt hid his disappointment. "Oh, well, have a fantastic time."

"How about Sunday?" Jake said, leaning in for a kiss. "I finish work around three. We could go for a walk or something."

Matt grinned. "I guess that's another date."

"I guess it is," Jake said, lingering over his lips. "I'll try not to miss you too much in the meantime."

"So will I," Matt said, knowing it would be impossible. He was already hooked.

Chapter Sixteen

Matt spent Saturday close to home. He'd done his share of active exploring in the previous days and wanted some quiet time to unwind. After a lazy breakfast, he made a large pot of coffee and spent the rest of the morning sprawled out on the patio sofa reading *Jaws*. He'd seen the movie several times but was surprised at how different the novel was from the film. And despite what Jake had said, he actually found the scenes at sea enjoyable, exciting even. Maybe it was the prospect of going for a trip on Jake's boat, but he got into the sea-faring adventure side of the story more than he'd expected to.

After lunch, he headed into the town and took the car. He needed to stock up on supplies from the supermarket, and it would be simpler to drive than make two or three separate trips over the next few days. The centre was busy, but he found a parking spot near the antique shop. Matt decided to go in for another look at the bronze and marble bookends he'd had his eye on the previous weekend. The heavyweight art deco panthers were even more beautiful than he remembered. They had a price tag of £950.

It was extravagant, but he was again taken by how beautiful and unique they would look in his flat in Leeds.

"They were made by Maurice Frecourt in 1925," the antique dealer told him. "They don't come on the market very often."

Oh, what the hell. He worked hard. What was the point of it if he couldn't treat himself now and then? At least he'd have something remarkable to show for it. Clinton would blow double that on the turn of a card without thinking twice. After a little haggling, Matt talked the price down to £875 and they shook on it.

The dealer packed them in bubble-wrap and into a large box. They were so heavy that Matt carried them straight back to the car. Now, as well as some amazing memories, he'd have a permanent souvenir of his holiday in Nyemouth.

He picked up more basic supplies of bacon, eggs, milk, cheese and booze at the supermarket. He'd decided on a quiet night in. Maybe he'd order a takeaway and make a start on the Harold Robbins book, now that he'd finished *Jaws*. Or he could watch a movie. After hearing about Dominic Melton and Arnie Walker's history in the house he was staying in, he was curious to check out some of Arnie's movies. Perhaps he'd queue one of them for a relaxing night in front of the television.

It was still early, so he took a short drive out of town rather than heading straight back to the house. He followed the coastal route to Seahouses and Bamburgh, driving with the windows down to enjoy the fresh evening air. It was after six when he arrived back in

Nyemouth. He wondered what Jake was doing as he turned onto South Bank Terrace. Probably getting ready for his night on the town, if he wasn't already out there. Matt hoped he had a great time and couldn't wait to see him again.

He parked around the side of the house and unloaded his shopping from the boot before carrying it up the garden path. It was only as he opened the gate that he noticed something was wrong.

There was a huddled figure on the ground, partly concealed by the rose bushes. He saw black shorts and a light blue T-shirt stained with blood. The figure lay on his side, facing away from him.

Matt's heart froze. His first thought was that Vince had gone too far with Jake.

He dropped the shopping bags and hurried to the figure.

As he noticed the solid, deeply suntanned legs, he realised it couldn't be Jake and relief surged through him.

Taking in the thick-set waist and the back of the broad head, he grasped who it was.

"Clinton."

The man on the ground groaned. Matt crouched over him and put a hand on his shoulder. Clinton flinched away from him, letting out a small shrieking sound.

"It's okay. It's me, Matt." He gently rolled Clinton onto his back.

Jesus. He was a mess. His face was almost unrecognisable. Both eyes were just about swollen shut. His nose looked like it was most likely broken. Blood and mucus dribbled over his chin. Matt tried to ease him into a sitting position.

Clinton let out a high-pitched scream.

"All right," Matt said, grabbing his phone. "Try not to move."

God alone knew how many broken bones he'd sustained. He looked like he'd beaten senseless.

Matt dialled for an ambulance.

* * * *

Three hours later, he sat with Clinton in the hospital emergency room. The injuries were less severe than Matt had imagined. His nose was indeed broken, as was his right eye-socket. He'd also sustained a fracture of his left wrist. Amazingly, none of his ribs were broken. Clinton had been dosed up on painkillers and sent for a full body X-ray. Now they were waiting for someone to reset his nose, stitch the cut across his forehead and put a plaster on his wrist.

"I didn't see anyone," Clinton explained. His speech was slurred, partly from the drugs but mainly from his busted lips. He'd also lost one of his front teeth. "They jumped me from behind as I came up your front path."

"They?"

"Two. There were two of them. I saw them once they had me on the ground and started kicking. Bastards."

"In broad daylight. That's incredible."

"They wore masks," Clinton said. "Kiddies' masks. You know, those plastic things with the elastic string around the back. One of them was Batman. I didn't recognise the other one. Another superhero, but I don't know who." Clinton put his hand to the side of his jaw as he spoke. The X-ray had shown that there was no fracture there, but despite the drugs, he was clearly in a lot of pain.

"Did they say anything?"

"Nothing. They just laughed. The whole time they were sticking the boot in, they just kept laughing. How sick is that?"

Matt sighed. Clinton's debts had obviously spiralled far out of control if it had come to this. Or he owed money to the wrong kind of people. It was a warning. The next time he would not be so lucky.

"What where they doing in Nyemouth? How did they know to find you here?"

"Must have followed me."

"And I take it you came here looking for money?"

"I'm desperate, man. You know I wouldn't bother you, but I have nowhere else I can go."

Matt didn't doubt it. Clinton had burned all his bridges when it came to people prepared to bail him out.

Matt shuffled his chair closer to the trolley where Clinton sat. "This has to stop," he said. "You can't go on living like this, crashing from one catastrophe to another. You used to be a respected, well-liked lawyer. Now you're getting beaten up in the street over your drug debts."

Clinton was racked with sobs. His shoulders shook. His eyes were too tight and swollen for Matt to see any tears, but he believed Clinton's remorse was genuine and not for show. Clinton had turned on his fake emotions too many times in the past to fool Matt with them now. "I know," he sobbed.

"How bad is it?" Matt asked. "How much are they onto you for?"

"Twenty-seven grand," he sniffled.

A lot of money, Matt thought, but Clinton had been down for much larger figures in the past, more than double that. It seemed strange that they would send the heavy boys after him now. Maybe circumstances had changed and he couldn't keep up the payments fast enough now that he was out of work — or maybe the debt had been sold on and the new moneymen were trying to make a point.

Matt didn't want to know. "I'll loan you the money," he said at last.

Clinton reached across with his one good hand. "Thank you," he sobbed. "Thank you so much, Matt."

Matt cradled his hand in his. "There are conditions."

"Anything. Anything you want."

"First off, it's a loan, not a gift. You have to pay me back."

"I will, I promise. Of course I will."

"Second, it goes to pay off what you owe and nothing else. I'll contact someone at the office and arrange for them to make the payment with you. I want to know for sure that your debts are clear."

Clinton nodded, though he looked less certain on this condition. "You can trust me."

"No," Matt stated, "I can't. I never could trust you, and that's why you're in this mess now. So, someone accompanies you to make the payment, or it doesn't happen. Got it?"

"Yes. Yes, of course."

"Okay," Matt said, sitting up straight. "And the third and last condition is that you seek help — not just for the drugs but for your gambling addiction and your financial management, starting right away. As soon as you get the money, you go into treatment."

Realistically, there was no way he could enforce that rule, but for the moment, while Clinton was filled with contrition, Matt wanted to hear him say it.

"I've always wanted to get clean. You know that."

A barefaced lie, but Matt let it go. Clinton had never been interested in professional help before. He'd always enjoyed the party lifestyle too much. He loved the booze, drugs and casinos, no matter how much trouble they landed him in. But things had never gotten this bad before.

"So, you'll agree?" Matt pressed.

"It's not like I have much choice," he huffed.

"Those are my terms. If you want the money from me, it's on the condition that you straighten yourself out. You're forty-one now, Clinton. You'll be dead long before you're fifty if you go on like this for much longer. There's still time for you to put your life back together. You could start living it properly again, instead of being afraid all the time."

Clinton squeezed his hand. "It would be worth it, if I knew you would wait for me afterwards."

Matt spoke softly. "We both know that's not possible. But trust me, it will be worth it, anyway. When you're clean and clear of debt, your life will be so much better. You'll meet someone else — someone you don't have to get high to have a good time with."

Clinton was quiet for a moment. Matt knew he was asking a lot of him. In reality, he'd decided to give him the money anyway, as long as he agreed to a chaperone to ensure it went to pay off his drug debts and wasn't wasted on more gambling and bad lifestyle choices.

"All right," Clinton said, at last. "I'll do it — rehab, counselling, whatever it takes. I don't want a life like this either."

Matt kissed the back of his hand. "I'll support you all the way. I'm proud of you."

Clinton attempted a grin, which came out as a grimace. "I'm damn sure I'll need it."

* * * *

Minty's stag party started at the working men's club on the south side of the river. Dominic, his best man, had offered to arrange a weekend trip to Blackpool for the celebrations, but Minty didn't want a fuss. This was his second marriage, and he wanted to keep things as low-key as possible.

Jake hadn't been around for Minty's first wedding some fifteen years ago, but it thrilled him to be invited to this one. It was a smallish group, mainly comprising volunteers from the lifeboat station. Dominic was there, obviously, and Joanne and Haig, Jacob and a couple of the ex-crew men who now helped around the station, together with Minty's two brothers and a handful of people Jake didn't recognise from his work. Although labelled as a stag party, they were an inclusive group with several of his female friends along for the ride.

Jake had initially been disappointed they would be staying in Nyemouth and would miss out on a boozy weekend in Blackpool. Things were different now, though, mainly because of Matt. As much as he'd have enjoyed a weekend away, he didn't want to spend two nights apart from him, not when Matt was only here for another week. Their time was precious.

Minty hadn't escaped the stag party experience entirely. Dominic had kitted them all out with identical T-shirts with his face blazoned across the front. There could be no mistaking their aim for the night.

After almost two hours, they hadn't progressed farther than the club bar. The atmosphere was merry, and everyone seemed content to order round after round of drinks in there.

It was an old-fashioned place, with a décor that hadn't been updated since the eighties. The prices at the bar were cheap, which he guessed was the main reason for everyone wanting to stay there. Jake didn't mind. It wasn't one of his regular bars, but it was friendly, fun and an ideal place for a low-key party like this.

He remembered a night several years ago, when, after a meal at The Lobster Pot, he'd playfully suggested to Vince that they cross over the river for a nightcap here. Vince had physically recoiled in horror at the idea.

"That dump," he'd said. *"Have you lost your mind? I'm not going in there."*

Jake laughed at the memory. Vince's snobbery had deprived him of so much pleasure in life. Jake doubted that Vince would ever change. Appearances were far too important to him.

"It's good to see you smiling again," a voice behind him said.

Jake was waiting to be served at the busy bar. He turned to find Dominic right beside him, a big, slightly drunk grin on his face. Jake had always had a soft spot for Dominic. For years, he'd held him up as the standard he looked for in a man. He was well built and darkly handsome, with deep, dreamy eyes and lush brown hair. Jake had never believed he'd find a man of his own who measured up to Dominic.

Matt Ramsey had changed all that.

"What makes you say that?" he asked, inhaling Dominic's sexy aftershave.

"Oh," he shrugged his big shoulders, "I don't mean anything bad. It's just that you seemed so serious all the time, especially since you split with Vince. But this last week, I've noticed a change in you. You seem happy. It suits you."

"Thanks. I am happy."

"Then I'm happy for you. Is there any reason for the change in circumstance?"

Sitting down across the room, Jake spotted Jacob Chisholm deep in conversation with one of Minty's brothers. Jake laughed. "I'm sure your old neighbour has tipped you off on what's happening."

Dominic's eyes crinkled. "Jacob might have mentioned something about a good-looking stranger renting my old place. He says the guy's really nice."

"He is. His name is Matt."

"You like him?"

"Yeah…a lot. We met last week, and he's only here on holiday, so I don't know what the future holds beyond the next few days."

"Worry about that afterwards. Make the most of those few days. If it's meant to go further than that, you'll work something out."

Jake sighed. "I get knots in my stomach just thinking about that. He's only here until next Saturday. I haven't even raised the subject with him. I don't know if he's thinking any further than that."

"The only way to find out is to ask."

"I know, but I don't want to spoil things. Then there's Vince. We're still married. He's opposing the divorce, so it could drag on for years. He'll go ballistic when he hears I've been seeing someone else, too. I just want to make the most of these few days with Matt while I still can. By next weekend, everything will change, anyway."

"I know what you're saying," Dominic said. "But don't let the past hold you back. Vince is a prick. You're better off without him. Everyone knows that. He can't object to the divorce forever. You'll get rid of him eventually. And things might work out with Matt, or they might not. You won't know unless you try. But one thing I know is, I've never seen you looking happier than you have this week. You deserve to be happy, Jake. Embrace it."

Chapter Seventeen

Joanne and Jake hauled the exhausted man from the choppy water, dragged him to the bow of the lifeboat with his ten-year-old daughter and began their first-aid assessments. Jake could see in an instant that the child was in a far better state than her dad. They had spent the last fifty minutes battling to keep afloat as the currents had dragged them from the shore almost a mile out to sea. The father had expended all his energy keeping his daughter alive until rescue had arrived. Now that they were on the boat, he was in far greater danger than she was of his body shutting down.

At the helm, Dominic turned the boat around and set a rapid course for the marina. Joanne got to work on the child while Jake focused his attention on the dad. He was conscious, but his responses were slow, and he seemed to struggle to focus on Jake when he spoke to him. Jake wasted no time in wrapping him in a foil blanket before checking his temperature with a thermometer in his ear.

"Twenty-nine point five," he shouted to Dominic, so he could radio the man's condition back to shore.

For the rest of the journey, Jake put all his effort into keeping the casualty alert and trying to raise his body temperature. He draped a woollen blanket on top of the foil. The man was shivering. *A good sign.*

"Can you tell me your name?"

"Y... Yohan," the man said. "Where's...where's Daisy?"

"Daisy is right behind you," Jake said, rubbing Yohan's shoulders. "She's doing brilliantly. She's even enjoying the ride, I think."

Yohan tried to smile, but his teeth chattered. He was talking and shivering, which was all good for Jake. He was in a moderate stage of hypothermia. He just had to keep him that way until they reached the shore.

Like last Sunday, the call had come in just as Jake was getting ready to finish his shift at the café. He'd been looking forward to spending the rest of the afternoon with Matt when his pager had gone off and he'd run to the lifeboat station instead. *Just as well the call didn't come in this morning,* he'd thought, when most of the crew had been hung over from last night's stag do.

The paramedics were waiting at the station and took charge of Yohan and Daisy as soon as they pulled the boat from the water. It looked like they would both make a good recovery.

Another satisfying rescue. Though they were definitely getting more frequent, as more of the tourists coming to Nyemouth got themselves in trouble on the beaches. Despite the warnings of high tides and dangerous currents, visitors to the coast were finding themselves in dire straits more and more often. Jake was just relived they had rescued two survivors from the sea and had not been looking to recover their bodies.

His mood brightened further as he spotted a familiar face in the small crowd of on-lookers who had gathered to watch the boats return.

Matt.

"Hey," Jake said, taking off his helmet and smoothing down his hair. "What are you doing here?"

"I saw the boat go out from up on the cliff. I thought I'd take a stroll down here and see what was happening. Did everything go okay?"

"Yes. Everyone is accounted for and back safely."

"Another heroic rescue. Someone ought to give you a medal."

Jake blushed. "We're just providing a service, that's all."

"How many times do I have to say it? You're a hero. You all are." Matt shoved his sunglasses into his hair and looked straight at him. "I can't provide you with the medal you deserve, but how does an ice cream sound?"

"Like heaven. I just need to finish up here. Can you hang on for twenty minutes?"

"For you," he winked, "I'd wait all day."

Jake floated through the station, taking off his safety equipment and kit.

This must be how it feels to have someone who genuinely cares about you and wants to make you happy.

Vince had never had the slightest interest in what happened during a rescue. More often, he would moan about how long it took and how Jake preferred to spend his time running after people he didn't know than staying home with his husband. Vince could be obtuse at times, but he'd got that part right.

"No wonder you've got that cat-who-got-the-cream expression on your face." Dominic stood in the doorway of the lifeboat station. He'd taken off his helmet but still wore the waterproof kit. He stared in Matt's direction. "So, that's him, is it?"

Jake took his elbow and dragged him away from the door. "Don't stare. I don't want him to think everyone is talking about him."

"They're not. It's only you and me," Dominic protested, a cheeky twinkle in his eyes. "I have to say, Jake, your taste has improved a million percent. He's a hottie, unlike the arsehole you married."

"I don't remember anyone bad-mouthing Vince when we were together," Jake said, taking his shoes from his locker.

"We did plenty, just never to your face. I wanted to put out the flags on the day you finally left him. You were always too good for Vince. You've got looks, personality, charm, a warm heart, bravery—all the things Vince lacks. But this guy, Matt, is it? On appearances alone, you're a much better match. You look like you should be together."

Jake groaned. "Don't jinx it."

"I said last night I was happy for you, and that was before I got a look at this guy. Now I'm over the moon about it. He's lovely—and so are you, so stop wasting time here and go out there and get him."

For the last year, since Dominic had met and settled down with Arnie Walker, the couple had become the marker for a solid gay relationship, something Jake didn't think he'd ever achieve.

Now, maybe that relationship goal wasn't as unattainable as it had seemed.

One day at a time, he reminded himself.

Matt was leaning against the railing, looking across the marina, when Jake came out. The view from behind was quite spectacular. Matt wore a pair of those snug-fitting chino shorts that hugged his butt and a navy T-shirt. Jake felt out of place in his black work trousers and polo shirt.

"Hey," Jake said, sliding up next to him. "Didn't someone promise me an ice cream?"

Matt leaned over to give him a quick peck on the cheek. Jake blushed.

"What's that for?"

"Because I couldn't resist you," Matt said. "Come on. How's the ice cream parlour over there?"

"It's great."

They fell into step together as they crossed the bridge to the other side of the river. Jake found a seat on the terrace while Matt went inside. He returned a few minutes later with two tubs of ice cream and two Diet Cokes.

"The ambulance took the man and the girl away before you came out," Matt told him.

"Good. They must be assessed properly. I'm pretty sure he was over the worst of it, but we're only trained in first-aid. They need proper medical attention."

"What happened? Did they fall in the water or something?"

"No, they were on the beach, just off North Point here, paddling in the shallows like a lot of people do. The little girl lost her footing and got carried out a little way. The dad went after her, but by the time he got her, they were both caught up in the currents, which took them straight out."

"Shit."

"Yeah. They were lucky there were people on the beach who saw it happen and called the coastguard straight away. The dad hung on to the girl and keep them both afloat until we found them. He was on the point of exhaustion. Another few minutes and it might have a been a tragic conclusion."

"Does that happen a lot? Not getting to people in the water in time?"

"The saves outnumber the tragedies by a long way, but one fatality is always one too many."

Matt leaned closer. Their legs touched beneath the table. "I had no idea it was so dangerous. These beaches all look so beautiful."

"They are, but the currents are deceptive. It can be as calm as a mirror on the surface, and it can still take someone unawares."

"You guys are just incredible. That none of you get paid for this is unreal."

"The service needs every penny it can get. We're always trying to spread the word and raise funds in any way we can. Summer fayres, Christmas, Easter, raffles, cake stalls… You name it and we're on it."

"You must let me know when the next event is. I'd love to get involved."

Jake nodded and licked his ice cream, trying to play it cool. That was the first sign Matt had given that he intended to maintain ties with Nyemouth once his holiday was over. He shouldn't read too much into it or build his hopes too high, but it held the promise that they had some kind of future together beyond the next week.

"I hope what you've heard this afternoon hasn't put you off going for a trip on my boat tomorrow," he said, guiding the conversation to safer ground. "The forecast is excellent."

Matt made a face then said, "It kind of depends."

"On what?"

"On whether you expect me to get in that bloody sea. I'll be fine and dandy on *The Golden Lady*, but if you're gonna chuck me into the water, the deal is off."

Jake threw back his head and laughed. Dominic had said he had never seen Jake smile as much as he had in the last week, but for Jake it was about how much he laughed when he was with Matt. He was quicker and funnier than any man he knew.

This was indeed something special. He didn't need Dominic to point it out. Having first-hand experience of a shitty relationship, he recognised how good things were right now.

"What do you want to do next?" Matt asked. "We could grab a drink somewhere."

"I had more than enough to drink last night," Jake remarked. "I'm just glad my head had cleared before the pager went off."

"Did you have a good night?"

"Yeah, we did. It was a lot of daft larking about, but it was fun. I suffered for it this morning, though. Getting up to open the café was no picnic, I can tell you."

"Poor baby," Matt said. "It's a nice night. We could go for a walk."

"I stink," Jake said, tugging at his polo shirt. "I've been frying bacon since seven. I need a shower and a change of clothes before I do anything."

Matt leaned closer. "I have a shower," he said suggestively.

"I know you do," Jake said, rising to the challenge. "And what about a change of clothes?"

"For what I have in mind, you don't need to worry about clothes."

"And how am I going to get home? Naked? Or do I have to put these stinky things on again?"

"I can lend you a pair of shorts and a T-shirt if you're shy about walking home naked."

"That's probably a good idea. Otherwise, I'll need to call on your services as a lawyer to help me out when I get arrested. You might not have noticed, but Nyemouth is not a bare-arsed kind of place. They don't take too kindly to that sort of behaviour."

"Really? And there was me, just beginning to like the place. If they can't appreciate a splendid peachy butt, maybe I overestimated the people here." He chuckled. "So, what do you say? Want to come up to the house for a couple of hours? I promise to get you home for bed in good time."

Jake stroked his bristly chin. "I think I'll take you up on that offer as soon as I finish my ice cream."

* * * *

Vince dialled Moody's mobile, and when he answered said, "You told me the job was done."

"Er…it is, boss," his lacky answered. "We kicked the shit out of the fucker. Left him in a real mess."

"Can't you do anything right?" he snapped. "I don't know who the hell you laid into last night, but I've got eyes on the target right now and there's not a scratch on him."

"No, boss. I swear it was him. We waited at the address until he showed up. He was just like you described him — dark hair, around forty, at that house. It was him. We got the right man. He should be in the hospital by now."

"I don't care what you say, you dingbat. I'm staring at the fucker right now and there's not a mark on him."

"I, uh, don't know what to say. Do you want us to take another pop?"

"And fuck it up again? Not likely. Just keep your mouth shut and I'll deal with this myself."

Vince hung up. *Stupid pricks.* They couldn't be trusted to do anything right. He should have known. Smashing up Jake's café was one thing, but expecting them to tackle anything more complicated than that had been a big mistake.

From the shade of an alley, he watched as Jake and Matt headed back across the bridge to the south bank. No prizes for guessing where they were going — up to that fuck-house at the top. And there was Jake, bold as brass with his new man. They might as well have held hands as they walked along and left everyone in no doubt as to what they were doing.

The disrespect was off the scale.

Matt was a smug cunt too. With that dark hair of his and his smarmy good looks, he thought he was such hot shit. He wasn't the kind of man Vince found attractive, but then Jake had clearly abandoned all his standards to jump into bed with Matt. He needed bringing down a peg or two and to be taught a lesson. No one had the right to swan into a new town and steal someone else's husband. And if they did, well, they had better be prepared to pay a heavy price.

Vince ground his teeth, thinking of all the things he'd like to do to Matt. He imagined throwing Matt and Jake from that high cliff up on North Point, like that guy had done last summer. Yeah, that would be a good way to deal with the problem. Seeing the pair of them smashed out across the rocks below, the tide coming in to wash their battered bodies out to sea... Jake was always blathering on about how much he loved the water. Let it have the pair of them.

Only the chance of getting them both up there together was slim. And if he did, he couldn't take them himself. They were both fit and strong and would overpower him before he had the chance to do any serious damage. He wouldn't be able to do it without the help of Moody and Curtis, and they'd already proved their incompetence. He couldn't rely on them again.

No. If Vince were going to take care of Jake and Matt, he'd have to do it alone.

The only way he could get them to do what he wanted would be by force.

Fortunately, he knew exactly what that would take.

They were gone now, had disappeared into the crowds on the other side of the river. That wasn't a problem. He knew where to find them.

Vince turned and headed down the alley. He'd parked on one of the back streets, far from the harbour. It was unlikely, but he hadn't wanted to take the chance on Jake spotting his car. He'd only come into town to see how Jake was handling the beating of his new boyfriend. He'd hoped to catch a glimpse of him as he left work, only the lifeboat had gone out on a call.

Typical Jake, he'd thought. He would put that damn boat ahead of anything.

Vince had hung around out of interest, still keen to see Jake when the crew returned, which was when he'd spotted Matt in the harbour.

Matt, looking fresh-faced and rested, not like a man who'd had the shit kicked out of him.

For a few seconds, Vince's vision had dimmed with fury. In a little over a week, he'd come to detest the man with every molecule of his body.

As Vince got in the car and headed home, a plan was already forming. His knuckles whitened as he gripped the steering wheel, and blood pounded in his temples. The doctor has warned him about his blood pressure, but Vince had refused to listen and wouldn't take the prescribed medication he'd been given. The only things that ever calmed him down were making money and getting his own way.

He'd known from the moment Jake had left him that he would never agree to a divorce, and nothing had changed there. If Jake thought flaunting another man in his face was the way to prompt him to sign, he was dead wrong. There were other ways to deal with a problem.

More effective ways.

Vince reached the modern mansion which had once been their family home. The house had been adapted to his precise demands. Jake was an idiot to have walked away from this. That dickhead lawyer might be fancy, but he would never amount to a house like this one. It was a veritable castle.

Vince went straight to his office off the central staircase.

Two years ago, he'd been involved in a deal with suppliers from Albania that hadn't gone to plan. The organised crime group behind the operation had made direct threats against Vince and his company if he did not hold up his side of the chain. For a while, things had gotten ugly, and Vince had seriously worried about how far they would go in their threats.

As a result, he'd sought protection of his own.

He unlocked the safe.

The Kel-Tec P-11 semi-automatic pistol had been his insurance. He'd acquired it from a gang in Newcastle and had been given basic instructions on how to use it. The trouble with the Albanians had blown over and Vince had never had cause to bring out the weapon. It had remained untouched in his safe all that time.

He removed it together with the three clips he'd bought, each holding ten rounds.

Vince had always been disappointed that he'd never been able to pull the trigger. He'd been curious how it would feel to point the pistol at someone's face and see the terror in their eyes.

He wouldn't have to wonder much longer.

With a grin, he inserted a clip into the gun and kissed the cold, hard barrel.

Chapter Eighteen

Jake yawned and stretched in Matt's arms, pushing his naked body against Matt's. "I had better make a move. It's almost eight. I really need to get some sleep tonight."

Matt wanted him to stay but didn't argue. After the stag party the night before, a full day at work today and a lifeboat call-out, Jake was on his last legs. "I'll drive you home."

"No. You don't need to. The walk will do me good. That last bit of exertion will mean I'll fall asleep as soon as my head touches the pillow."

"If you're exhausted, we don't have to take that boat trip tomorrow. We've got the rest of the week."

Jake tickled him around the ribs. Matt yelped and rolled across the bed.

"Nice try, but you won't get out of it so easily," Jake said, chasing him and coming in for a kiss. "Besides, there's nothing like sea air to blow the brain fog away. I can't wait to get back out there, and tomorrow looks the best weather day by far. The rest of the week doesn't sound so great."

"Typical. No doubt the sun will return with a vengeance when I go back to work next Monday."

"Try not to think about that yet. You're still on holiday and need to make the most of every day."

Matt intended to, and that meant spending as much time with Jake as he could, even if it was at sea in a small boat. With Jake at his side, nothing could go wrong.

Jake slipped out of bed and wandered naked to the bathroom, allowing Matt to admire his fine fuzzy butt. He almost had to pinch himself to believe it was real. He had never been so into another guy, both physically and emotionally. As well as being the bravest and most interesting man he had ever known, Jake was hands down the hottest.

Clinton had been a handsome man in his day, before the excesses of his lifestyle had taken their toll, but he'd never been that well-rounded. Matt had had more meaningful conversations with Jake in a week than in all the years he'd known Clinton.

He hadn't told Jake about what had happened there yesterday. With all the crap Jake had going on with his own ex, Matt didn't want to worry him with Clinton's problems. He intended to get onto the bank in the morning and arrange a transfer of money from some of his investment accounts. It would probably take a few days to release the cash, but he was confident he could have Clinton's massive drug debts cleared by the end of the week.

Clinton didn't deserve another handout. Matt had done it one too many times before, but he couldn't bear to see him beaten again. If he could resolve this problem and get his ex-husband onto a treatment programme for his addictions, Matt would draw a line under their relationship. Part of it was unresolved guilt for not dealing with Clinton's issues when they were still together, but Matt had now paid for that several times over. If he were to move on with his own life, that couldn't mean constantly raiding his savings to make up for the past.

Matt got out of bed and pulled on his underpants. He opened the wardrobe and took out a fresh pair of shorts and a T-shirt.

"Clean clothes, as promised," he said, when Jake came back into the room, still naked, his soft cock swaying with each step.

"It's not necessary. I was joking earlier. You only brought a set amount of clothes."

"And there's a washing machine in the kitchen, so I won't go short on clean stuff. Take them. We're close enough to the same size that they should fit you."

"Okay," Jake said, raising his hand to cover another yawn.

"It's time you were in bed. You're exhausted."

He nodded. "I am pretty wiped out…but in a good way. I've had a lovely afternoon with you."

Matt took him in a soft embrace, rubbing his cheek against the side of Jake's. "I have too. The best. And thanks to you, a little girl and her dad are safe and alive tonight. You really are amazing."

Jake kissed him on the ear. "You keep saying that, but a rescue is a team effort, not just one person."

"You and the entire crew are amazing. You're an inspiration."

"It's nice to hear you say that."

Jake put on the clean clothes he had given him, while Matt pulled on what he'd been wearing earlier. Matt went downstairs, leaving Jake to gather up the rest of his things. It pained Matt that Jake was leaving, but he didn't want to show it. He was a young man with his own life. Matt knew better than to get clingy with him.

He wandered barefoot to the fridge and poured a glass of white wine. There was cheese and ham in there. He was debating whether to just make a sandwich for himself or order a takeaway when Jake came down the stairs, covering another yawn.

"Are you sure you don't want me to drive you home? You look dead on your feet."

"I'm positive. I enjoy walking, especially when it takes me through the harbour." He came in for another hug, letting his chin rest on Matt's shoulder.

Matt held him, this beautiful young man who had brightened his life in a matter of days.

"Give me a quick call or a text when you get there, just so I know you're safe."

Jake squeezed his butt. "Yes, mother."

Matt laughed. "Sorry. Too much?"

"Actually, I kind of like it." He gave his arse another pat. "Okay, I will."

Matt walked him to the door, and they had one last kiss on the step. "See you tomorrow. Sleep well."

"And you. I'm looking forward to it already."

Jake waved from the end of the garden path before walking down the lane.

Matt watched him until he was out of sight.

"Isn't that just cute," Vince muttered. The brief wave Jake shot to his lover as he minced away made Vince want to stick his fingers down his throat.

He stood at the gable end of the terrace, out of sight. He'd been there for twenty minutes, waiting to see what happened. In that time, no one had come walking by in either direction, which was perfect. He'd dressed down in case they spotted him, in dark jeans, a black hoodie and one of Jake's old baseball caps — the kind of shit he wouldn't be seen dead wearing. Unless a passer-by happened to know him well, they could never identify him.

He checked the time. It was after eight. How long had they been in there? It must have been about five when he'd seen them leave the harbour. Three fucking hours they'd been at it. And there was Jake, wandering away without a care in the world, oblivious to who might see him. Gossip was rife in a piss-ant little town like Nyemouth. Everyone must know by now that Vince's husband was fucking the hot tourist.

He had no shame.

Vince ground his teeth and jerked his hips, savouring the cool pressure of the pistol in his jeans pocket. He had never carried the gun on his person since acquiring it. He'd been crazy not to. Just the weight of the weapon against his body gave him a stiffy, harder than he'd gotten for any man recently.

He'd had no plan when he'd left the house with the gun. What he'd have liked to do was shoot Jake and Matt in their smug faces, but he wasn't stupid enough for that. He couldn't, not without setting up an alibi in advance, and he had no idea how he was going to do that. It wasn't like getting a dumb stooge to break Jake's windows while he was away on business in Amsterdam. This was one task he couldn't rely on someone else to do for him.

No, this time the pleasure would be all his.

Since acquiring the gun, he'd always been curious about what it would be like to set it off in someone's face. He'd fantasised about the moment, and although he'd been relieved when tensions had de-escalated between him and the Albanians, part of him had been disappointed that he wouldn't get to use his new toy. He'd thought about taking it out somewhere, maybe off into the woods or moorland where he could practice on an animal, but the risk was too great. The weapon was illegal, unlicensed. If some farmer caught him blowing holes in his sheep and called the police, Vince would be looking at a long stretch inside.

So he'd bided his time. Waited for an opportunity.

Like tonight?

Could be.

Maybe he wouldn't have to pull the trigger. Just the sight of Jake's husband with a shooter might be enough to scare Matt away. He'd probably shit himself, pack his car and fuck off back to wherever the hell he came from.

But would that be enough for Vince?

This man was banging his husband. Anger tore through him just thinking about the two of them together, having the kind of sex Jake had denied him for the last few months they'd been together.

They had tried to make a fool of him and needed to be taught a lesson.

Keeping close to the wall, Vince traced the line of the building, looking for a way in. The rear wall went all the way up the rock-face of the cliff behind and there was no route in — no back passage or gate. Undeterred, he looked at the top of the wall. It was maybe seven or eight feet high. *No big deal.* He took a few paces back to see what he could make of the property beyond. It was a typical two-storey terrace house of the type seen all over the old town. Dominic Melton appeared to have replaced all the windows as part of his refurbishments on the property.

Vince smiled, realising his luck was in.

The frosted window of the bathroom on the upper floor was open. It would be a squeeze, but he was as snake-hipped now as he'd been in his early twenties. He could make it through there without a problem.

Checking there was no one coming in either direction, he took a running jump at the wall, and, with a bit of scrambling, hauled himself onto the top. The yard below had been decked out as some kind of naff patio with lounge furniture and a table. The back doors to the house were closed.

Vince was in a precarious position. Should someone come by, walking their dog or taking an evening stroll along the cliff, they would spot him straight away. He shuffled along the wall until he came up against the edge of the house. The window was a stretch, but he reached it on his second attempt, opening it farther.

Luck continued to shine on him. The bathroom was empty. Matt must be in some other area of the house.

Vince hoisted himself onto the sill. The window was tighter than it had appeared from below, but he made it through with little effort. He had missed his vocation. If his ambition to become a multi-millionaire businessman had fallen through, he'd have made a first-rate burglar.

He paused in the bathroom and held his breath. Though his pulse raced from the effort it had taken to get up here, his nerves were steady. Excitement coursed through him rather than apprehension. This was easy. He'd made it into the house without being seen, like a villain from a cool movie. He wanted to laugh, but that would only have drawn attention to himself.

Surprise would be his biggest weapon against Matt. He had to use it wisely.

Matt put on some music and fixed a rum and Diet Coke before checking the cupboard to see what he wanted to eat. Spending time with Jake had caused him to work up a mighty appetite, but he decided against another takeaway. Between the restaurant meals and the take-outs, he would be the size of a house before the end of his second week if he weren't careful.

There was ham, cheese, salad and bread, so it would have to be a sandwich. He got out the chopping board and set about assembling what he would need. Just as he was grating the cheese, his phone rang. *Jake.*

He snatched it from the counter and answered.

"Hey, you."

"Hi. Just letting you know I'm home."

He grinned. "You could have just texted."

"I wanted to hear your voice one last time before I turn in."

Now he beamed. It seemed so silly, and he would have laughed at someone else for being overly sentimental, but it was wonderful to hear Jake say something like that. "I'm glad you did. It's good to hear you too."

"I'm beat, though. I'm going to bed in the next twenty minutes. I want to be fresh for our trip tomorrow."

"I'm looking forward to it. Where shall we meet? Do you want me to come to the boat?"

"Yeah. I just want to call home to change after work and pick up a few bits we might need. How does two-thirty sound?"

"Perfect. Two-thirty at *The Golden Lady*. I'll see you there. Sleep tight, Jake."

The Golden Lady.

From the upper landing, Vince did well not to laugh out loud. *Are they serious?* They planned to go out on that clapped-out bucket of Jake's. He'd forgotten about the old boat, thinking Jake must surely have gotten rid of it by now. It was older than he was. Matt must really think a lot of Jake if he was prepared to risk his life on that piece of shit. It was good for nothing but the scrap yard.

They sounded very cosy with each other on the phone, which only angered him more. Hearing the way Matt spoke to Jake, all lovey-dovey… Had they really only met for the first time last week? The more Vince thought about it, the more unlikely it seemed. Jake must have been lining this guy up for some time. Maybe it had only been online until now, but there had to be a history beyond what Vince knew.

That scheming little whore. No wonder he was so determined to press ahead with the divorce. While Vince was doing all he could to save what they had left of their marriage, he was screwing around.

Vince ran his fingertips across the shape of the pistol in his pocket. He shuddered and moved them down the outline of his erection next. He had the power to shatter their lives for good. They thought everything was perfect. He would teach them otherwise.

Would shooting Matt tonight really be the answer?

It couldn't do any harm. It would teach Jake a lesson for certain, and as long as no one saw him leave the house, he was sure to get away with it. He could even call Pete, that hot little chicken from the warehouse, over for the evening. Vince was certain he would come. He'd just have to make out that he'd been home, thinking about him all afternoon, then fuck his tiny brains out. It would give him a good enough alibi for the time of the shooting. Pete was too dumb to ask questions and would surely say anything Vince told him to.

Yes. The problem of Matt can be resolved here and now.

Vince licked his lips in anticipation.

Noise would be a problem. The gun had no silencer. He could only afford a single shot. One of the neighbours would dismiss it as a car backfiring or gunfire on TV. That would mean close range, which would not be a problem. He wanted to be right beside Matt when he pulled the trigger. He wanted to see the life go out of those smug eyes.

Surprise would be his best chance. He'd wait here until Matt came upstairs, then jump him. Shove the pistol in his face before he knew what was happening. If Vince went downstairs, he might alert him. The floorboards up here seemed pretty solid. They had probably been replaced, but he had no idea about those stairs. How much would they creak when he stood on them? These old places made plenty of noise.

No, better to wait here. Unless there was a downstairs bathroom, Matt would have to come up soon enough.

Matt was smiling so much that it made eating the ham and cheese sandwich difficult. He didn't have all that much of an appetite any more, anyway. All he could think about was Jake. He even looked forward to getting back into bed later and sleeping with the young man's scent on the pillows. It wouldn't compare with having him there for real, but it would give him some small pleasure until they met again tomorrow.

Matt realised how bad he had it. It had never been his intention to fall for Jake. He'd spent most of the first week trying to avoid him and convince himself he felt nothing for him. There was no denying it now. He had it bad—feelings far deeper than anything he'd experienced before. The simple fact was that he was smitten and loving every second of it.

A knock at the front door interrupted his thoughts. Matt pushed the half-eaten sandwich away and got up to answer it, surprised to discover Jacob from next door.

"Jacob, how are you? Is everything okay?" His immediate assumption was that the old guy must be ill or needing help with something in the house.

"Yes, I'm fine," he said, his sharp blue eyes twinkling.

It occurred to Matt for the first time that Jacob must have been a very handsome man in his younger days. Those eyes were electrifying. And though that thick head of hair was now pure white, he could only imagine how luxurious it must have been in his prime.

"Is there anything I can do for you?"

"Well, there is. But before I ask, I want you to know that I won't be offended if you refuse. It's quite all right."

Matt stepped forward, putting him at ease. "This sounds intriguing."

"It's just that I bought a nice bottle of Scotch a couple of weeks ago—single malt, 38 years old. Probably around your age, I would guess. And it's not much fun drinking alone. Whiskey always tastes better in company, I find. I used to get through a good few bottles with Dominic when he lived here, but since he moved across the river, I don't see him as much as I used to. I just wondered... If you aren't doing anything, would you like to come next door and enjoy a few tipples with me?"

Matt gazed at him in delight. "What a lovely offer."

"As I said, I won't be offended if you say no."

"I'd absolutely love to. Thanks for the invitation. No one has ever asked me in like that before. Living in a city, people are not so neighbourly. Do you want me to bring anything?"

Jacob looked happy and relieved. "Just yourself."

"You got it. Give me a minute to grab my shoes."

Shit.

Vince slipped back into the bathroom as Matt came bounding up the stairs. He looked around, grateful to discover that there were no shoes in there. Still, that didn't mean he wouldn't call in there before leaving the house. If he did, it would force Vince to shoot him *and* the stupid old man, none of which fit into his plans.

Matt thudded along the hall to his bedroom.

Vince stood on the toilet seat and climbed onto the windowsill.

Getting out without making a sound seemed so much harder than it had coming in. He squeezed through the opening, hanging on tight to the frame. One wrong move now and his plans would be in greater trouble than they already were. Whatever happened next, he'd have to come back to wipe his damn prints off everything he'd touched there. It had been stupid of him not to wear gloves. When something happened to Matt, the police would be sure to dust the place.

Vince hit the top of the wall and leapt straight to the ground below. His ankle jarred painfully on impact, and he swore under his breath. He checked the path in both directions. The sky was darkening, but there was no one around.

He'd made it.

No thanks to that nosy old man. He'd forgotten Jacob lived in the house next door. Part of him had been certain Jacob was dead, but he must have been wrong.

The old man had bought Matt a reprieve, but it would not be for long.

He would get Matt tomorrow. He was determined. And if Matt and Jake were heading out in that boat of his, maybe he could deal with two of his problems in one strike.

An idea was already forming. Maybe it was a good thing they had foiled him this evening, because the alternative plan was so much better.

He'd get rid of them, and no one would suspect anything other than a tragic accident.

Chapter Nineteen

Though The Seagull Café was busy, Monday morning was a complete drag for Jake. It should have been his day off, but as summer was a peak time for them and the previous Monday had been busy, he'd volunteered to put in some extra hours. He couldn't keep his eyes from wandering to the clock, counting off the minutes until he finished work and could be where he really wanted to be...with Matt. When they were with each other, the time flew by, but when they were apart, it seemed endless.

Though he'd been loath to leave Matt's bed yesterday evening, he'd actually slept very well last night, aided in part by the most wonderful and sexy dreams. Physically, they might have been at opposite ends of the town, but Jake felt as though he'd done nothing but make love with Matt all night long. It was the perfect way to be apart.

Usually the time flew by when the café was busy, but he'd never known it go as slowly as it had today.

When the clock finally crept around to eleven, he smiled. *Only one hour remaining.*

He had checked the weather forecast and things were looking good for this afternoon. There was a light south-easterly wind, a moderate swell and temperatures were in the high teens. *Perfect conditions.* He didn't want Matt's first experience on his boat to be spoiled by heavy seas. He knew Matt had to overcome a lot of apprehension to join him, and he wanted it to be as faultless as possible.

Just as Jake finished plating up a chicken salad, Sandra came through from the front and said, "Vince is here again."

She spoke under her breath, but not quietly enough to prevent his sister from hearing. "What the hell does he want? Tell him he's barred."

"It's okay," Jake said. "I'll deal with him."

Vince was actually the last person he wanted to see today, but he didn't want him loitering around into the afternoon and potentially spoiling his special time with Matt. Better to deal with him now and get it over quickly. "Where is he? Outside?"

"No, he's having a coffee."

"Sandra," Lizzie bellowed, "why the hell did you serve him? He knows he's not welcome here."

"Sorry," Sandra said. "He's in a good mood. Polite, even. I've never seen him make an effort like that before. I thought one cup of coffee couldn't hurt."

"I'd have pissed in the damn coffee if I'd known," Lizzie chuntered.

"Don't worry," Jake said, taking off his apron. "I'll get rid of him. This won't take long."

Vince sat at a table by the window. He was dressed casually, which put Jake on immediate alert. Why

Thom Collins

wasn't he at work? If he was on leave, Vince would never spend time in Nyemouth. He hated the place. Jake couldn't help but think of the other night, when Vince had turned up at the house just before his first proper date with Matt. It was almost as if he knew when they had plans together, which was impossible.

"What can I do for you?" he asked, approaching the table.

"Nice job they made of this," he jerked his thumb towards the new windowpanes. "Nobody would ever know."

"Is that all you came to say? As you can see, we're busy. I've got a lot of work to do."

"Sit down," he said jovially. "It can't hurt you to take five minutes off. You always did work too hard. How many times have I told you so?"

Sandra was right. He was being nice...totally unlike himself. It put Jake even more on guard.

"Why aren't *you* at work?"

"I've taken a few days off. I also work too hard. The place can manage without me for a little while. I've got things I need to take care of."

"Such as?" Jake asked, wary. Vince was up to something. He'd known him long enough to recognise the signs. He was never as pleasant as this unless he had an ulterior motive. He'd always boasted about the way he liked to do business—charming his clients and suppliers, while screwing them for everything he could get. This felt like exactly that.

"Sit down, please. People are watching. They don't all need to know our business, do they? It's personal."

Jake sighed but pulled out a chair and sat across from him. "Strange place to choose if you want to talk in private."

"You wouldn't have agreed to see me any other way. Admit it. Oh, it's all right. I don't blame you, especially after the other night. I shouldn't have said the things I did. I was upset. I didn't mean it." He made a theatrical show of blowing the froth on the top of his coffee before sipping.

"I'm listening now," Jake said, then added. "But my time is like my patience — short. So, what is so important today that it just can't wait?"

"All right, if you want to be like that. I came to tell you I've got an appointment with my solicitor tomorrow. Eleven o'clock." He paused for dramatic effect. "I'm going to sign the divorce papers."

"You are?"

"Don't look so surprised. Isn't this what you want?"

"Yes. Of course, it is." He studied Vince's face, looking for the tell-tale signs he was lying — or, more likely, just taking the piss. Vince was a master at winding people up. "But…what changed? You were adamant last week that you wouldn't. Why today?"

He rubbed his chin, dragging out the time before he answered. "I suppose I've just had time to think. I woke up yesterday morning and asked myself what I was going to gain by holding things up. You don't want me anymore. I get that. But I held on out of spite and kept us both from moving on. It's time to draw a line under it, don't you think?"

Jake couldn't tell if he was being genuine or not. He'd never known Vince to be this unreadable. He was saying the right things, so he couldn't argue with that. "Okay. Well, if you see your solicitor tomorrow, we can take it from there."

Vince took another elaborate sip of coffee, then said, almost coyly, "I might have met someone."

"You have?

He nodded and gave a giddy smile. "I don't know. I don't even know if he likes me back. It's a guy who works at the warehouse. They call him Pete. He flirts with me, and I flirt back. I think there's something there, but we haven't taken it any further than that." Another affected pause. "He's only nineteen."

Jake tried not to laugh. Did Vince want him to be impressed or jealous? All he felt was pity for the poor kid, if any of this were true. Young and naive, just the way he'd been when Vince had come along, only Pete was in a worse situation. If he worked for Vince, he would have no kind of independence.

"It sounds like you're ready to move on," Jake said, getting to his feet.

"I sure am."

"Then I'm glad for you. Dragging out the divorce doesn't make either of us happy. Speak to your solicitor tomorrow and I'll call mine later in the week."

He went back to the kitchen. The last thing he wanted was to listen anymore. He couldn't shake the feeling that this was nothing more than an elaborate set-up.

"What did he want?" Lizzie asked as she put a chicken breast on the grill.

"A divorce, apparently," Jake said, putting his apron back on.

"You're joking."

"No. But I'm not convinced he isn't."

Her mouth tightened. "I wouldn't trust that bastard as far as I could throw him."

"Me neither. Once he's signed the documents, I'll believe him. Until then, I'm wary of anything he says. Don't you think the timing is strange? He has resisted for over a year, and now that I've met Matt, he's all for it. That's not the way Vince works. If he knew I'd been seeing someone else, he'd dig his heels in even harder."

"Maybe he's met someone himself."

"He says he has — some kid at the warehouse."

"There you go then. Let some other poor sap have him. As long as it gets him out of your life, just roll with it."

"Yeah, I know. It's just that, well, I've known him for long enough to recognise when he's up to something. He's saying all the right words, but they're not convincing." Jake looked distractedly at the next order. "And I don't care what he says. The more I think about it, the more certain I am that he was behind the broken windows here. So, last week he arranges to have the café trashed, then today he comes in all sweetness and light, telling me everything I want to hear. Something's not right."

Jake tried to put Vince out of his mind and finish his shift. He had his sea date with Matt to look forward to, and there was nothing Vince could do to spoil that.

When he finished at The Seagull, Jake hurried next door to The Lobster Pot. He'd arranged an order with Kelly before going to bed the previous night. He wanted to make the afternoon with Jake as romantic and perfect as possible.

Kelly greeted him with a hug at the counter. "It looks like you've got a beautiful day for it," she said, indicating the blue skies outside. Sunlight glimmered on the still water of the marina. "Are you excited?"

"Very," he admitted. "I've got butterflies already, just like I did the first time we went out."

"That's wonderful. I'm jealous. There's nothing quite as exciting as the feeling of new love."

"I've never experienced this before. I mean, things were good in the early days with Vince, but they were never like this." He put his hand on his sternum. "In here... I never felt it here with Vince. But with Matt, there are moments when the strength of those feelings threatens to overwhelm me."

"Wow. It sounds like you've got it bad."

"Do you think I'm rushing into this?"

"Do you?"

"Not really. It all feels so right. But then I'll get this rush of pure emotion that I don't understand. It's amazing, but it's also a little frightening — to be taken by something so strong."

Kelly grinned. "You're in love."

"You think?"

"Don't you?"

"Yes, but I don't know what love really feels like, so I'm confused too. I don't mean the kind of love I have for you and Lizzie, family love. This is something very different."

"I should think so. It's passion. It's how it feels to fall head over heels for someone, like the most euphoric drug. And you can't think or concentrate on anything else."

He nodded. "That pretty much sums it up."

"Then enjoy every second of it. That kind of intensity doesn't last. If you're lucky and things progress further between you, a more mellow but stronger love will develop with time. But for now, grab that pure emotional high and make the most of it. Don't be scared of it. It's something wonderful."

Jake inhaled. She was right. He had fallen deeply in love with Matt. It wasn't something he could deny or hide from. Just because he'd waited until he was twenty-six to experience this kind of emotion didn't mean he should ignore it.

Jake gathered up the takeaway parcel. He would see Matt again in less than an hour. He needed to get home to shower and change before their little cruise for two.

* * * *

Vince was not happy at the way Jake had brushed him off. *The ungrateful shit.* All he'd blathered on about for months had been the damn divorce. He should have been sucking Vince's cock with joy that he'd agreed to sign the papers, not dismissing him and pissing off back to the kitchen.

Still, it had done the trick. He'd noticed the old women at the next table eavesdropping on their conversation. And he was sure the couple behind him had been listening too. Jake would have told his bitch-sister about his offer the second he saw her. There were enough witnesses to prove Vince bore him no hard feelings and was moving on with his life. He really had made an appointment with his lawyer for the next day, too, not that he would need it. The divorce would be redundant by then.

Vince wore a humourless grin as he opened the boot of his car. He'd parked on the clifftop on the south side of the river, where there was no CCTV coverage. The car would have to stay there for most of the day, but he doubted anyone would pay it much attention. There were plenty of other vehicles around, belonging to hikers and walkers and people just too cheap to pay the expensive parking rates in the town centre.

In the back of the car was his leather holdall. He pulled out a plain navy hoodie he had bought at a supermarket that morning. It would be burned sometime tonight, and if he were lucky, no one would ever see him wear it. Next came a stainless-steel hip flask, filled with vodka. Something to keep him warm when he needed it. He shoved it into his jeans pocket then looked around, making sure there was no one nearby to see him.

The Kel-Tec P-11 was at the bottom of the case, together with a spare clip. Vince's heart quickened as he looked at it. He couldn't believe he had kept it hidden in a safe all this time. If only he'd guessed how much pleasure looking at and holding the gun could give him, he'd have taken it out years ago. Maybe if Jake had known about it, he wouldn't have been so quick to pack his bags and leave. All Vince would have needed to do was threaten to use the gun on the bitch-sister and Jake would have stayed a compliant little pup, instead of the arrogant whore he had become.

Vince ran his fingertips over the cold gunmetal and a shudder scurried down his spine. His cock roused in his pants.

If touching the gun had this effect on him, he could only imagine how great it would be to pull the trigger.

The ultimate power of life or death in a single twitch of his finger.

Vince groaned deep in his chest. *Not long now.*

He grabbed the weapon and stuffed it into his right hip pocket, where the muzzle pressed against his balls, and he put the spare clip in his back pocket. It was unlikely he would need it, but running a successful business had taught him to be prepared and plan for every eventuality. He shut the boot and locked the car.

It had just gone one o'clock. *Time to get a move on.*

He'd heard Matt say he would meet Jake on *The Golden Lady* at two-thirty.

From where he had parked, it would be a good fifteen-minute walk to the marina.

Vince put on his shades and set off at a brisk pace.

Chapter Twenty

Matt chose his clothes with care, wanting to look his best for Jake. He opted for light blue shorts, a navy polo shirt and a dark hoodie. Though it was warm in the front garden, the temperature was bound to be cooler once they left the shelter of the harbour. He'd been down to the supermarket that morning and bought a bottle of chilled Moët and a pack of prepared tapas. He'd stored them both in a picnic cool box, ready for their afternoon voyage.

Surprisingly, he didn't feel any nerves or apprehension about going out on a boat. He was far too excited at the prospect of spending the day with Jake.

At ten-past-two, he put on his blue Converse shoes, picked up his shades, carried the cool box outside and locked the front door. He tied the hoodie around his waist and set off down the path.

Jacob waved to him from his front garden, where he sat on a deck chair reading a paperback novel. "Have a lovely time."

"Thanks, Jacob. Catch you later," he said, waving back.

Matt had slept soundly all the way through until ten that morning, thanks to Jacob. They had sat up together until after midnight the past night, drinking his fine whisky. Matt had felt guilty drinking so much of his good stuff, but Jacob wouldn't hear of it, insisting he was glad for the company. Matt intended to pick up a special bottle for him as a thank-you before the end of the week.

He'd expected to wake with a terrible hangover this morning, but instead, he felt well rested and fresh. *Maybe it's only the cheap stuff that gives me a hangover*, he mused.

His anticipation levels rocketed when he reached the bottom of the lane and turned into the marina. Jake had given him directions to where his boat was moored and he found it easily, spotting Jake on the upper deck of the craft as he walked onto the jetty.

"Good afternoon, Captain," he called as he approached.

Jake looked up with a million-watt smile on his face.

Matt took in *The Golden Lady* for the first time. "Whoa, hold on. You told me this was a small motorboat. I was expecting one of those little tubs with an engine on the back."

He didn't know much about boats, but this looked like a big, fancy motor yacht. To start, it was huge, looking like fifty feet from the gleaming white front to the back. There was a large cabin area with a flying bridge on top, which was where Jake was standing.

"I don't think I said she was small. She's pretty old, though." Jake climbed down a ladder on the rear, open deck.

"She doesn't look it." He couldn't see a scrap of rust anywhere on the boat. He appreciated the hours and love Jake obviously put into his pride and joy.

"Well, don't just stand there. Come on aboard."

Matt handed over the picnic box before stepping onto the back of the boat. Jake came straight in to greet him with a kiss. Matt gasped as he saw through a set of double doors into a large, carpeted saloon area with a leather sofa and two armchairs. "I never expected this. Wow."

Jake grinned. "I supposed I'm so used to it that I don't really think about it anymore. When I first left Vince, I lived on here for a couple of weeks, until Lizzie insisted I move in with her, so I guess there is plenty of room. Come on. Let's put this stuff in the fridge and I'll show you around."

"Fridge? You see, I didn't think you'd have one of those. That's why I brought the cool box."

"It's nice, being able to surprise you."

They stepped inside to the lounge.

"Jake, this is beautiful."

The boat might have been old, but she didn't look it. Jake had taken a lot of care in modernising the interior. At the far end of the room, he saw a neat kitchen area. The carpets looked new and so did the furniture.

"I can actually sleep six people here," Jake said. "Down below there's a main stateroom with a double bed, then two smaller bedrooms. One's a twin and the other has two fold-down cot beds, and there are two bathrooms and a shower."

"So, this is a proper holiday yacht."

"When my parents were alive, we had some fantastic holidays on her. One year we did a complete circuit of the British Isles. We went to the Shetland

Islands, Isle of Man, Devon and Cornwall. It was incredible. Vince wouldn't entertain the idea of even spending an afternoon onboard, so the farthest she's been in years is an hour or so up and down the coast. I'd love to take her on a proper voyage again someday."

Jake opened the fridge to put the supplies Matt had brought in there. Matt noticed it was almost full already with white containers.

"What's all that stuff?" he asked.

"It's a surprise," Jake said. "For later. Unless you're hungry already."

"No. I had a late breakfast."

"Perfect. Let's get going first. I want to get you out to sea before you change your mind."

"That won't happen. I'm far too excited to back out of this now."

Jake took a beer from the fridge and gave it to him. "Here. Relax and enjoy it. Let's go up above. The view from the flying bridge as we leave the harbour is the best."

Jake untied the mooring ropes and Matt following him up to the open top deck. He watched Jake, full of admiration, as he took the wheel and edged the boat away from the jetty. Within seconds, he completed a one-eighty-degree turn in the harbour and pointed the boat towards the mouth of the river.

Matt felt a sudden pang of anxiety as they approached the open water, but he ignored it. He could be in no safer hands than Jake's. This extraordinary young man grew more remarkable the more he got to know him. Matt trusted his expertise.

As the boat exited the piers at the mouth of the river, a slight list from one side to the other became apparent, but it was less pronounced than he had expected. Once clear, Jake turned north and increased the speed. A fresh wind tore at their hair. It was even more invigorating out here on the water than it was from the shore. Matt breathed deeply.

"See that house up there, at the top of the cliff?" Jake pointed to the large dwelling on its own.

Matt shielded his eyes against the glare. It looked old, like a small manor house with a surrounding wall. "Yes."

"That's where Dominic lives with Arnie Walker. And just under that" — he pointed to the beach and rocky outcrop below. "That's where Arnie and his son got into trouble last summer. It's a dangerous piece of shore. Visitors don't appreciate how fast the tide comes in there and how soon they can become cut off. We've been involved in a fair number of rescues from that beach over the years."

He kept the boat heading north.

"So where are we going?" Matt had to shout to be heard above the wind and the engine.

"A little way up the coast. There's a nice bay. It's secluded and difficult to reach without a boat. I thought we could go ashore and have a picnic on the beach. You can take a swim if you like, though I wouldn't recommend it. The water here is freezing, even in the summer."

"Yes to the picnic, no to the swim. You've warned me enough about the dangers in the water here, so I'll pass on that," Matt said. "I didn't bring a swimming costume, anyway."

Jake looked at him sideways, his cheeks dimpling as a grin spread over his face. "We'll be the only people there, I'm sure of it. You won't need swimming trunks."

Matt gave his butt a playful slap. "I like your way of thinking, but it's still a no on the swimming. It's one thing to get me in a boat, but it's something else to get me in the water."

Jake's expression became serious. "If it bothers you, I've got some life-jackets. Maybe you should put one on, anyway."

"Relax, I'm fine. I have no intention of going anywhere near the edge. I'm not going to fall in."

Matt opened the beer and turned his face into the wind, enjoying the bracing sensation. Every few minutes he would steal a glance at Jake, who looked magnificent as he stood at the wheel, his feet spread wide, butt all tight and high, his dark hair whipping about his head. He looked so handsome and mature far beyond his age. Despite the thirteen years between them, today Matt felt like the junior partner in their relationship, putting himself completely in Jake's capable hands.

It seemed like they'd been going for about an hour when Jake steered the boat towards the shore and into a small cove. He eased right back on the engines.

"Here we are," he said. "I need to anchor offshore. I can't get the boat any closer than this, but I have a small outboard dinghy that will get us to the beach and back."

Without the propulsion of the engine, the yacht wallowed in the gentle swell, tipping more dramatically from side to side. It took some getting used to, but Matt didn't find it as unsettling as he'd thought he might. He kept a firm grip on the ladder as he followed Jake back down to the main deck and found he had to take a wide stance when moving around to keep his balance. Other than that, he found the motion quite relaxing.

"I won't be able to take everything in one trip," Jake said. "How about I put you ashore with the picnic table and chairs, and while you set them up, I'll scoot back here for the food and drinks?"

"Whatever you say, Captain," he said with a salute.

The journey to the shore was just as exhilarating as the trip there, as Jake sped him to the beach in the small dinghy. The sand was pristine and golden in the warm afternoon sun. A high rock cliff rose about two hundred feet above it, and Matt could see that Jake was right in his assessment that the only way to reach this place would be by sea. It was a deserted oasis on the rugged Northumberland coast. Matt would never have found the cove on his own.

He unfolded the table and chairs and set them up above the tideline, together with a broad sun umbrella. The equipment must all have belonged to Jake's parents, he figured. With Vince unwilling to let the poor guy use the boat to its full potential, Jake would have had no need to splash out on replacements.

Jake returned a few minutes later, carrying a basket laden with goodies. Matt admired the way his chunky thighs rippled as he came bounding across the sand. He handed Matt the bottle of champagne and two long-stemmed glasses. "Why don't you open that while I set out our lunch?"

Matt watched in amazement as Jake opened Tupperware containers and laid out the contents on the table. A bowl of shelled giant prawns, a rice salad, cold cuts and pasta.

"Are those what I think they are?" Matt asked, as Jake put down two fat pieces of succulent white and red flesh.

"Lobster tails," Jake said. He opened another container. "And the claw meat. I figured we wouldn't want to be messing around trying to shell them on the beach."

"Don't tell me…The Lobster Pot."

"Got it in one. I asked Kelly if she'd prepare it all this morning. Picked it up when I finished my shift."

"You've gone to so much trouble," Matt said, thinking his contribution of champagne and tapas seemed meagre in comparison.

"It's no trouble at all when it's for you," Jake said. "For *us*. I wanted today to be perfect. Besides, you're my guest. I invited you, so I wanted to make it special."

Matt pulled him in for a kiss. "It was already special. Being with you is the only treat I need."

Jake pressed his lithe young body against him and kissed him long and deep. "Thanks for coming. It means so much to me."

"Hey," Matt said, rubbing his cheek against the side of Jake's face. "I told you, I wouldn't have missed it. I don't want to waste another moment of this week without you."

The food was excellent. The lobster was succulent and rich, and tasted wonderful with the dry champagne. Matt realised how easily he could get used to eating like this and had to remind himself that he was on holiday. These were treats he couldn't expect all the time—and yet he wanted to. There was a conversation he needed to have with Jake, and he didn't know which way it would go. He decided to wait until they had finished their lunch before raising it.

The champagne disappeared too quickly, but Matt had no sooner poured the final drops when Jake reached into the cool bag and produced another.

"Great minds think alike," he said, peeling off the foil wrapper. "Though I can't have too much of the second bottle. I have to drive the boat back."

"Are you trying to get me drunk?" Matt asked.

"As drunk as you want."

"Then I'll go easy too. I want to remember this day when you've put so much effort into it." He accepted the refill on his glass. "There's something that's bugging me, and I figure I might as well get it out of the way now."

"That sounds ominous," Jake said, putting the bottle back in the cooler.

"It depends on how you look at it." He took a deep breath. "So, Friday is my last full day in Nyemouth. I'll be heading back home on Saturday morning."

Jake nodded, grimly. "I know. I've been trying to ignore that fact."

"So, the question hanging over us is, where do we go from here? I don't want this to be a fleeting holiday romance. I know you've got a lot going on in your life right now, and I don't want to do anything that will make things harder for you. If you're happy to close the book on what we have here at the weekend, well, I won't like it, but I'll understand."

"No," Jake exclaimed. "That's the last thing I want."

The tension Matt had been holding eased in an instant. "Really?"

"Absolutely." He leaned across and took Matt's hand. "Listen... My life is a bit of mess right now, but

I'm not going to throw this away because my ex-husband has been dragging his heels. Vince came into the café this morning. He claims he has an appointment with his lawyer in the morning to sign the divorce papers. I don't know if I believe him or whether he's playing mind games, but I'm not going to let him ruin this."

"So where does that leave us? Nyemouth and York aren't exactly close."

"We'll come up with something. They're not at the opposite ends of the country, either. Other couples manage with distance between them, so we'll just have to do the same. We can take turns to see each other at weekends and see how it goes from there."

Matt pressed his lips to the back of Jake's hand. "You've no idea how much it means to me to hear you say that. I didn't know if you'd be interested in a long-distance relationship."

"Are you kidding? After spending so many years in a shitty marriage, I know a good thing when I see it. I won't let a small thing like travel put me off. Besides, York is a straight drive down the A1 from here. It's not like it's a tough ride. I'll speak to Lizzie and rearrange my shifts so I'm not working every weekend, especially during the winter. If I finish work around three on a Friday afternoon, I could be in York by the time you're through for the day."

Matt beamed with raw emotion. There was nothing else for him to worry about. He could relax and enjoy the rest of his holiday, knowing there was a future for him and Jake beyond this weekend.

They spent the remainder of the afternoon on the beach, grazing on the food and champagne, taking about all the things they would do together. Matt felt like he'd known Jake all his life, while at the same time discovering everything new about him.

"We should head back," Jake said around six o'clock. "There's a change in the tide and the swell is more pronounced than on the way here. I don't want to spoil your day by making you ill on the homeward journey."

"It's okay. I think I have my sea legs by now."

"I like your confidence."

They packed up the picnic stuff and Jake ran the furniture back to the boat before returning in the dinghy for Matt. When Matt stepped back onboard *The Golden Lady*, he realised what Jake had said about the swell. The boat performed a long roll from side to side, and Matt had to grab the handrail to hold his balance.

"I'll steer her back from the pilot house," Jake said. "It's probably a bit too windy for the flying bridge."

They went through into the saloon and Jake continued straight ahead to the wheelhouse. He started the engines, and as soon as the boat got underway, the roll became less pronounced.

"Why don't you finish off the champagne?" he suggested. "There's only a glass or two left in the bottle. Enjoy it."

"Thanks," Matt said, taking the bottle out of the cooler and removing the rubber stopper Jake had stuck in the top. "Are you sure you don't want any if it?"

"No, I've had enough for now. I need to keep a clear head. Don't want to crash the boat into the jetty."

Matt laughed. "I guess not. I'll buy you a glass in The Fisherman's Arms to make up for it."

"That's a deal."

Jake slowly turned the boat around and set off on a course heading south. An offshore wind had come up across the afternoon and whipped up white crests on the increasing waves. Matt found the dramatic change in the weather on the homeward route rather exciting. He knew he was safe in Jake's expert hands.

"Well, hasn't this been a cosy fucking day at the beach?" said a voice from behind.

Both men spun around.

Vince appeared on the stairs that lead to the lower deck, his head and shoulders rising as he climbed upwards.

It was only when the top half of his body came through the hatch that Matt noticed the gun in his hand.

Chapter Twenty-One

Jake didn't see the gun at first. When Vince had appeared from the lower deck, Jake's immediate thought was to wonder how the hell he'd gotten on board and how long he'd been there. Vince couldn't have boarded when they were on the beach. He must have snuck on before they'd set sail, and as Jake had only unlocked the boat when he'd arrived around two, he couldn't figure out how Vince had done it.

Then he saw the pistol. He wondered if it was just a harmless replica, but only for a second. Vince had often boasted about the gangsters he knew in the city, how they would make any of his problems disappear if he only asked. For years, Jake had written off the claims as bullshit and exaggeration on Vince's part, but one glimpse of the gun and the anger burning in Vince's eyes, and he knew they were true.

"I didn't quite believe it when I heard you intended to come out in this old tub," Vince said, displaying the dismissive attitude he had for anything that didn't interest him. "I'm amazed this piece of shit still floats. But it looks like you've had yourselves quite the little pleasure cruise. Picnic and champagne on the beach... It would be sweet if it wasn't so damn sickening. Do you know how many hours I've been waiting down there?"

At a loss for what else to do, Jake eased back on the speed and switched on the autopilot to continue their course. He turned towards Vince with his hands raised. "What are you doing here?" He kept his voice low, placatory, the way he'd learned to after years of living with this man.

"Spoiling the party, wouldn't you say?" His thin lips drew back from his teeth. "Yeah, I bet I'm the last person you expected to see after you walked away from me this morning, nose stuck in the air like you're too good for me. That's a laugh, right? The thick-as-shit yokel trying to lord it over me – the man who fucking made you."

"Nobody is lording anything," Jake said, sounding calmer than he felt. "You said you were going for a divorce, and I believed you."

"You believed me because it suited your agenda. It made it nice and easy for you to sail off into the sunset with old blue eyes here. Well, here's a newsflash for you. There won't be any divorce because when I'm finished here today, there'll be no marriage left."

Icy fingers skittered along Jake's spine. This was not one of Vince's usual hollow threats. He'd already crossed a line in getting the gun. Vince was all in on his craziness.

"Vince," Matt said, "don't do anything hasty. You have done nothing yet that you can't walk away from. It's not too late."

Vince pointed the pistol straight at Matt. Jake noticed the way his hand trembled and prayed there was a guard on the weapon. Vince's itchy fingers could set off that trigger in a second.

"Hasty? You don't know who you're dealing with, mate. If I were hasty, you wouldn't be here now. I'd have blown your brains out when I was in your house last night." He laughed. "That's right. How do you think I knew about this trip? I heard the pair of you on the fucking phone. I was right there at the top of the stairs, listening. If that old fart from next door hadn't come knocking at the door when he did, I'd have taken care of half my problems then and there."

Jake looked at Matt. His hands were raised and, though his mouth was tight with tension, he appeared to be holding it together. Jake's mind raced, wondering what the hell to do. As long as Vince was talking, it kept him from carrying out whatever he intended. He'd always loved the sound of his own voice, especially when he had something to brag about. Their best hope for now was to keep him talking.

"How can it have come to this?" Jake asked. "Eh? You can't take everything you've worked so hard for to risk it now—the house, the business, the cars. Is avoiding a divorce really worth all that? You know our relationship hasn't been good for a long time."

"We were fine," Vince snapped. "If you hadn't paid so much attention to that bitch sister of yours, we would still be together. You changed when you started listening to her."

"No, I changed because I grew up. I wasn't the same the person at twenty-five that I had been at nineteen. I became a man, but you wanted to keep me as a boy, asking you for money and permission to do my own thing. That's not how it's supposed to be."

"You ungrateful shit," he spat. "I did everything for you. I gave you whatever you wanted. And you threw it back at me so you could take up with the likes of this twat."

"We were finished long before Matt came along. You knew that, Vince. You had to. It was obvious to everyone. It doesn't mean it has to end like this. I don't mean you any harm. I never did."

"Then you should have thought of that before." Vince looked out of the cabin window. "Where is this heap heading now?"

"Back into port."

He nodded, a whole new mien of spite settling on his face. "Keep going until you're past the river mouth, over to the south shore."

"Okay." *What the hell is he planning?* Jake figured if he kept the speed down, he could drag that out for a good hour. He had no idea what he would do when they got there, but at least it bought them some time. It meant Vince wasn't intending to use the gun just yet. He took up the wheel again and turned off the autopilot.

Now they were further out, the swell was noticeably greater.

Poor Matt. He'd talked the guy into taking this trip when he didn't want to come. Now it had turned into a disaster, thanks to Vince and his jealousy. Maintaining the lower speed would cause the boat to wallow in the waves, but it couldn't be helped. It was the only way to delay whatever Vince had in mind.

Vince moved closer to the kitchen. "Get over there," he said to Matt, waving the gun in Jake's direction. "I want you both where I can see you."

Matt did as he was told, keeping his hands in the air, stumbling for balance as he crossed the saloon towards the pilot area. Jake fought to keep the boat steady against the swell, thinking all the time about what he could do to talk Vince out of this dire situation. He knew there was not a lot of hope. Vince had always been pig-headed, and once he set his mind to something, there wasn't much anyone could say to dissuade him otherwise. Even when it meant disaster for himself, once he was set on a course of action, he would stick to it.

Which made their current situation even more deadly. Vince had gone to the trouble of getting a gun, which meant he had some mad idea in mind.

"Where did you get the weapon?" he asked.

"Are you hoping it might be a toy?" Vince said with a laugh. "Want to put your theory to the test? It's real, all right. You know I have contacts who can get me anything I want."

Matt looked at Jake, seeking confirmation. He gave a curt nod.

"Your problem," Vince continued, "is that you have always underestimated me. Too busy caring about your café and that fucking lifeboat to concern yourself with anything at home. This" — he waved the pistol — "has been in our house for years, right under your nose. I could have used it whenever I wanted. That would have sorted out our marriage problems in an instant."

Cold fingers of dread curled around Jake's insides. He'd always known Vince had issues, even at the start of their relationship, when he'd presented a veneer of perfection, but he'd had no idea just how dangerous the man he'd been living with could be — not a clue. Their marriage had been an even bigger sham than he'd thought.

"It's not too late to put this right," Matt said. "You can throw that thing over the side and we'll just pretend we never saw it. No one else will ever know but the three of us on this boat."

"I'll put you over the fucking side if you make one more stupid suggestion," Vince said, waving the gun in Matt's direction. "I didn't come all this way to just roll over and just do what you say, Mister-fucking-perfect. Maybe a bullet in your knee will teach you who you're really dealing with."

"Vince," Jake pleaded, "please stop waving that thing around. We're doing everything you ask of us. No one needs to get hurt."

Vince chuckled. "Yet."

Jake shot Matt a warning glance to say no more. He didn't want him to give Vince a reason to lose his tenuous grip on control. If he used that gun, he could only imagine how trigger-happy he would become. He drove on in silence, wondering about their best move.

If they could get Vince out onto the open deck, there was a slim hope of getting the gun from him and throwing it over the side. Here in the cabin, the chance of success seemed greatly reduced.

Vince picked up the bottle of champagne Matt had left on the counter and glanced at the label. "I might have known. Cheap supermarket piss. You two have no class." He took a long swig from the bottle, watching them all the time.

The boat passed the mouth of the river Nye. Instead of turning into port, Jake steered on as Vince had requested. They were about three-quarters of a mile off South Beach. He reduced the speed.

"We're here," he said.

Vince glanced out of the window, seemingly surprised that they had reached their location. "We are?"

"There's the south cliffs right there." Jake pointed.

He nodded, looking even more twitchy than before. "Cut the engine and drop the anchor."

Jake did as he asked, wondering what the hell he had in mind. Surely his plan wasn't to shoot them here, so close to shore. They would wash up on the next tide. Besides, Vince had no idea how to drive the boat back to harbour, and if he did, how would he explain it when they were found with his bullets in them?

It made little sense, but nothing about this situation did. Vince was not thinking like a rational person. Jake had to remember that.

Vince wiped the back of his hand across his mouth. "All right. Outside. Both of you."

"What are you going to do?" Jake asked.

"Blast the pair of you right here if you don't do what I fucking say." His eyes widened, showing white all around the iris.

"Vince, come on. This has gone too far," he pleaded.

Vince pointed the gun at the ceiling and fired.

In the close quarters, the sound was like an explosion. Jake and Matt ducked, while Vince looked startled by the power of the weapon and noise it had made. His face twisted into a perverse grin.

"Fuck me. Whoa." He laughed, loud and hysterical. "Get the fuck outside before I finish this here and now."

Jake rose and nudged Matt's elbow, urging him to follow him out onto the open deck. Wind whipped at their hair and threw up spray from the water. The weather was changing, deteriorating in a way that hadn't been forecast.

Vince came out of the cabin, wielding the gun like the madman he so obviously was. He pulled something out of his pocket and tossed it to Jake. He missed, and it fell to the deck.

"Pick it up," Vince said.

Jake stooped, realising what the item was — a long strip of plastic, a cable tie.

"Bind his hands behind his back." Vince gestured to Matt.

"No way. This is insane."

"Do it," he barked.

"Vince, no. You can't be serious about this."

He raised the gun to the level of Jake's face. "Don't I look like I'm serious? How else is the fucker going to sink unless his hands and feet are tied?"

"That's mad. How do you expect to get away with this? It's murder."

"I'm at home right now, getting cosy with my little boy toy. I'm not stupid. Of course I'll be the first person the police call on, but I'll have an alibi sewn up tight."

"No one is going to lie and cover for you — not for murder."

"People will do anything if you offer a big enough incentive, like a large house and lots of spending money. You might have thrown what I gave you back in my face, but I think little Pete is going to take to his new lifestyle very well. And he'll be grateful for it, unlike you. Now tie the fucker up."

The boat rocked from side to side. Jake widened his stance and stood up straight to Vince. "Not a chance. If you want to kill us, you'll have to do it yourself."

Vince's face was a blank mask. Not a trace of emotion showed on its surface.

"Fine," he said.

He swivelled and pointed the gun at Matt. Before either of them could react, he pulled the trigger.

There was an explosion of sound and a burst of blood as the bullet impacted Matt's upper thigh. The force took Matt clean off his feet, back towards the port-side rail, just as the boat took another deep roll in the swell. Jake leapt towards him, grabbing for his legs as he flew through the air.

Too late.

The power of the blast and the motion of the vessel sent him straight over the side and into the sea.

Chapter Twenty-Two

The shock of submersion in the cold sea caused Matt to inhale, drawing in the salty water. He kicked for the surface, coughing and retching as his head came clear. The pain in his leg was secondary as his instinct to survive kicked in. He heaved and cleared his airway enough to gasp a breath of fresh air.

He could not see the boat and spun around in the water, trying to get his bearings. He was lifted on the next swell, and when he reached the peak, he saw *The Golden Lady*, much more distant than he would have thought possible.

"Jake," he yelled before he slipped down into the next trough, and when he rose again, the boat was even more distant. He realised he must be downwind of them, being carried away with each second.

Jake was still on the boat, with Vince and the gun.

Vince had shot him. The thought only registered now. He'd pointed the gun straight at him and pulled the trigger. The man was a psychopath, much worse than either of them had ever imagined—and he had Jake.

Matt leaned into the water and tried to swim.

He could feel nothing of his right leg. There was no pain, but the fact that he could gain no propulsion made him fear the worst.

Another swell rose beneath him, and at its crest he saw the boat. Even more distance had opened up between them. He screamed as loud as he could but knew they would not hear him. The wind would carry the sound in the wrong direction. Matt slid back into a trough and saw nothing but sea. He slipped beneath the surface. Holding his breath this time and managing not to swallow any water, he struck upwards in the direction of the light.

His fear for what was happening onboard outweighed his concerns for himself. What did Vince intend to do to Jake? He'd been hiding below deck all afternoon, stewing with hate and anger, no doubt getting off on his gun fantasies. Why hadn't it occurred to either of them that he could be dangerous, that he'd have a weapon? A firearm—the penis extension of choice for ineffectual men the world over.

Vince had come on board to kill them. There was no doubt about that, not after the way he'd casually pulled the trigger on him. What would he do to Jake now? Shoot him? He'd intended to tie Matt's hands and throw him to the sea. Did he have a similar fate in mind for his husband, the man who had scorned him and his fragile ego? No. Vince would have a far worse fate in mind for Jake.

Don't think about it.

He had to get back to the boat before it was too late.

Matt leaned forward and tried to swim again. His limbs were even less effective than before.

So cold. He'd only been in the water a few minutes, but the cold had taken hold. His entire body quivered. His limbs were leaden, and his teeth chattered.

Undeterred, he struck out again. He would not give up on Jake without a fight.

When Matt went over the side, Jake climbed onto the side of the boat, ready to jump in after him. Vince grabbed the tail of his shirt and hurled him back onto the deck. Jake landed heavily, smashing his shoulder against the steps to the pilot bridge. He ignored the pain. All that mattered was saving Matt.

"Relax," Vince said, his voice placatory, as though he hadn't just shot the man Jake loved. "It's just me and you now, the way it's supposed to be."

Jake cowered against the step, letting Vince think he was more badly hurt than he was. "What have you done?" he asked, sounding meek and timid.

Vince came nearer. "I did it for us—all for us. That man tried to destroy our relationship, but he's gone now. We don't have to worry about him ever again."

Jake put his hands over his face, pretending to cry. *Come on, you bastard. Come closer.*

Vince moved right on top of him. "Don't worry. It's going to be—"

Jake balled his fist and slammed it into Vince's groin with all the force he could muster.

Vince howled, and the gun clattered to the deck. Jake slipped out from under him and grabbed the weapon then hurled it into the sea.

That evened the score.

He turned on Vince, who was holding his groin in both hands. *Pathetic.*

Jake hurried to the port side and looked out for Matt. There was no sign of him in the water around the boat. The swell was high now. It would carry him south.

"Matt," he bellowed. "Matt. Make a sound if you can hear me. Let me know where you are."

Suddenly Vince's weight was on top of his shoulders, dragging him.

"What part of 'he's gone' don't you understand?" he growled, slamming his fist into the soft space beneath Jake's ribs.

Anger threatened to consume Jake. He hauled back with his elbow, hitting Vince in the belly. Vince grunted and loosened his hold. It was all Jake needed. Years of frustration, of being worn down by this man, erupted. He spun around and smashed his fist straight into Vince's face. Vince turned his head, and the blow glanced off his chin.

"Is that all you've got?" he taunted. "I'm going to give you the kind of beating I should have done years ago."

Vince flew at him, but Jake was quick, ducking out of the way of his punch, before getting in one of his own, into the soft flesh of Vince's gut. Unable to contain himself, Jake swung again and again, smacking into Vince, driving him backwards. Vince got in a fist of his own, hitting Jake full in the face. Jake was not about to give in to him now. He drove Vince closer and closer to the starboard railing until Vince backed right up against it.

"It's time you found out how useful the lifeboat really is," Jake yelled.

One shove was all it took, and Vince toppled over the railing and vanished beneath the surface.

Jake did not wait to see what became of him. He scrambled up the ladders to the pilot bridge. He switched on the engine, and as he waited for the anchor to rise, he radioed the coastguard, giving their position.

"Two casualties in the water," he said. "One of them has been shot. Request immediate assistance from the Nyemouth lifeboat, coastguard helicopter and paramedics on standby at Nyemouth station."

Without a care for what had become of Vince, Jake steered the boat around and headed steadily south, knowing the tide had to have taken Matt in that direction.

* * * *

Matt felt more alone than he had in his entire life…completely. Each time he was caught on the rise of a wave, he ceased swimming and raised his head above the water, looking for the boat. Nothing. He had lost all sight of it.

How far had he drifted? He had no idea. The boat was gone, and the shore seemed farther away than ever.

He gave up shouting for help. It was a waste of energy, and every time he opened his mouth, he seemed to swallow more water.

Swimming became increasingly difficult. He could no longer feel his legs, and his arms were getting weaker every second.

He remembered a survival technique. He couldn't recall if it was something Jake had told him about or something he'd seen on TV, but he rolled onto his back and concentrated on floating. No more swimming, no great bursts of energy, just float and try to keep his head above the water.

He could not do this indefinitely. Sooner rather than later, the cold sea would take him. His only chance was for someone on one of the cliffs to spot him and alert the coastguard. The chance of that was negligible. He was too far out. Nobody would see him there — but for now, his hope held out.

He would not give up.

Each moment he survived was a moment closer to rescue, and rescue meant justice. Yes, he would bring Vince to justice for what he'd done. The man deserved to spend the rest of his life behind bars, and if Matt made it out of this, he would make sure it happened.

He didn't want to think about what Vince had done to Jake. He wouldn't allow his thoughts to go there. Vince was a monster, the worst kind of criminal he'd encountered — petty, self-absorbed, merciless. Well, Matt would be ruthless in tracking him down.

He would stay alive for as long as possible so he could spend the rest of his life hunting the bastard.

Matt's anger tapped into an unused reserve of energy. Though his jaw shuddered and his arms were rapidly losing all sensation, he treaded water and kept afloat.

Vengeance... That was what he wanted. Not for himself, but for what Vince had done to Jake. Jake was the most wonderful man in the world, and Vince had spent years abusing and betraying him.

Matt would make him pay.

As he floated farther out to sea, hatred kept him alive.

* * * *

From the pilot bridge of *The Golden Lady*, Jake scanned the water. Years of experience had taught him how difficult it was to spot a person in the water, even in the best conditions, let alone on seas like this. Difficult, but not impossible. He'd done it before, and he would do it for Matt.

He refused to accept the idea that Matt had gone. Vince's bullet had hit him square in the thigh. It was a critical injury, but not immediately fatal. In the cold water, it soon could be, but Matt had a chance. About fifteen minutes had passed since he'd gone in. Survival times in the water here could be anything from five minutes to over an hour, depending on the temperature and sea conditions, but that did not take into account an injury like Matt's. But if he conserved his energy and tried to stay afloat rather than swim, he had a better-than-average chance.

Jake glanced over his shoulder and saw the Nyemouth lifeboat tear out of the river mouth. The coastguard helicopter had yet to arrive. He hoped the lifeboat would join him in the search for Matt. Vince hadn't been shot. His chances of survival were far greater. *Let the bastard wait.*

He continued to scan the water ahead.

"Where are you, baby? Please hold on until I find you."

Jake eased back on his speed. Allowing for the wind speed and current, Matt couldn't have drifted much farther south than this—not in the time he'd been overboard.

Jake watched the shifting, swelling waves. The conditions were worsening as the afternoon wore into evening.

Suddenly, there was something. *Up ahead, nine o'clock position.* Jake increased his speed and turned in that direction, easing back when he came close. He watched.

Nothing but water.

God damn it.

He cut the engine.

"Matt," he shouted into the wild, open water. "Matt, it's Jake. If you can hear me, please make a sound. Call out so I can find you."

He waited, listening. Wind moaned around the structure of the boat.

"Jake."

He turned to the starboard side.

The voice came again. "Jake. Over here."

A dark shape appeared on the crest of a wave, about twenty yards ahead.

Jake bolted into action, dropping the anchor and sliding down the stairs to the deck below. The dinghy was tied to the back of the boat, trailing in the wake. He jumped onboard and started the outboard motor, tearing out to where he'd seen Matt last.

The small craft bumped on the unexpected swell and Jake immediately eased back on the speed so he didn't capsize. He would be no use to Matt if he ended up in the sea himself.

He moved closer, frantically searching the ever-moving surface of the water.

There he is.

Jake's heart hammered. Matt was not out of danger yet, but he was alive for now. Jake forced his emotions aside and concentrated on his training and experience. The only way out of this for both of them was if he acted like a professional and not a lover.

He drew the boat alongside and stopped the engine.

Matt was on the verge of exhaustion and hypothermia. Jake recognised all the signs.

He reached down and hooked one arm beneath Matt's shoulder, grabbing his shirt with the other. He was a dead weight. Matt tried to haul himself on board the dinghy, but there was no strength remaining in his limbs.

"Stay still," Jake told him. "Let me do all the work."

With a mammoth effort, Jake heaved Matt half over the side of the small boat. From there, he got a firmer hold on his shorts and pulled him all the way in.

His skin was freezing. His lips were blue.

Jake shook his shoulders. "Can you hear me, Matt?"

He gave a weak nod.

"Good. I need you to stay awake, okay? I'm taking you back to the big boat, but please honey, do not fall asleep."

Jake needed to get him warm and back to shore as soon as possible. He pulled Matt close to him so he could share the heat of his own body and gunned the outboard motor again, turning the small craft back towards *The Golden Lady*.

Epilogue

Nine months later

It was a beautiful day in Nyemouth, much like it had been for the whole of the previous summer, when Matt rolled his suitcase along the marina, passing in front of the lifeboat station, heading for the end dock. Matt pulled the heavy case with ease, and the limp he'd suffered since Vince had shot him was barely noticeable now. After months of physiotherapy and strength training in the gym, the pain was greatly reduced.

He had wondered, in the days afterwards as he recovered in the hospital, whether he would feel the same about this small seaside town, whether some of the love he felt for the place would have died. He had no doubts about Jake. Jake had remained at his side for as long as the doctors and nurses would allow him to. If they hadn't insisted he leave each night, Matt was certain Jake would have slept in the chair beside his bed.

Any doubts he'd had about Nyemouth had vanished the moment Matt returned. Dominic Melton had offered the use of the cottage on South Bank Terrace rent-free for his convalescence. As Matt had sat in the front garden, his leg raised and supported in front of him with Jake at his side, he'd realised there was nowhere else he would rather be.

Nyemouth was not responsible for the actions of Vince Ashfield, and Matt bore no grudge against anyone or anything other than Vince.

Vince had been fished out of the North Sea around the same time that Jake had rescued him. Matt's memories of the first few hours were fuzzy as he was treated for the effects of hypothermia and given surgery to remove the bullet that remained lodged in his thigh. Jake had filled him in on the details afterwards.

Vince had denied any knowledge of what had happened to Matt. He'd denied ever being on board *The Golden Lady* in the first place and claimed he'd been swept out to sea by a freak wave on the beach. His bullshit story didn't hold up for a minute, especially not when the police found a round of cartridges in his safe that matched the bullet removed from Matt's leg. Fingerprints and DNA also proved he'd been on the boat, together with witnesses who had seen him board it in the harbour. Jake had figured Vince must have had a copy of the key made at some point in the past.

Vince had initially been released on bail, pending further investigation, with conditions in place that he was not to enter Nyemouth or contact Jake or Matt in any way. But as the evidence against him had mounted, he'd been charged and remanded into custody. He'd continued to deny all charges made against him, and the case had gone for trial at Newcastle Crown Court in March.

The trial had lasted three weeks. Jake and Matt had been required to give evidence. Matt had coached Jake as best he could on what to expect. Vince's barristers had come at him from every angle, dissecting their relationship and marriage in minute detail, presenting all the ways that Vince was a model husband and Jake a cheating, mercenary spouse. The attack had convinced no one, not when the case against Vince was so strong.

Even his two heavies, Moody and Curtis, had testified against him on the condition that they would be exempt from prosecution afterwards. Then it had all come out how Vince had paid them to trash The Seagull Café, and about when he'd ordered them to beat up Matt, they had attacked Clinton in error.

Matt had felt even more guilt over that, but Clinton had been sober for seven months and counting, and had even started a small repayment programme to give back the money Matt had loaned him. Clinton had insisted he bore Matt no ill will, and though they'd been mistaken about the reason for his attack, it had shocked him into making positive changes in his life.

Vince had been found guilty on all charges against him — attempted murder, grievous bodily harm and possession of an illegal firearm. The judge had sentenced him to life imprisonment. Watching from the public gallery, Matt had smiled grimly. *Life inside...* Vince deserved nothing less.

Now Nyemouth was his home. Jake had negotiated with his crew mate Dominic for them to buy the house on South Bank, and they had moved in together just a month before. Matt had given notice at the solicitors he worked for in Leeds and put his flat on the market. Later this summer, he would open his own law firm right here in town.

But first, he had something more important to do.

As he rolled the suitcase to the far dock where *The Golden Lady* was berthed, it surprised him to find a small crowd of people gathered by the yacht.

They cheered him as he approached.

"Surprise," they called.

Of the familiar faces, he saw Lizzie and Kelly, Jacob, Dominic and his husband Arnie. They smiled and waved flags as he came closer.

"You didn't think we were going to let you go without a proper send-off, did you?" Jacob asked.

Matt laughed and looked for Jake. He was already on board, grinning from the stern. "I had no idea about this," he said. "Honestly."

Matt was flooded with emotion. These people were proof of the love and support he'd found in Nyemouth. Small towns had a reputation for being frosty towards newcomers, but they had welcomed him with wide open arms from the start.

"Here... Let me help you with that," Arnie Walker took the heavy suitcase and lifted it from the dock onto the boat. Matt had become good friends with Arnie and Dominic in the last few months, and they had been on several double dates together at The Lobster Pot.

"I've got you something for the voyage," Jacob said, handing him a boxed bottle of whisky. "It will help keep the chill at bay on those cold nights at sea."

Matt thanked him and shook his hand. "And I'll pick you up a bottle of something special when we reach Scotland. We'll enjoy it looking at the stars when we get back."

"I'll look forward to it. Safe trip."

Matt climbed from the dock onto the boat. Jake was waiting with a steady hand. He looked like a true sailor, in navy shorts and a blue-and-white striped sweater. Excitement was clear in the dazzling depths of his eyes.

"All set?" Matt asked.

"Ready when you are."

"Let's go."

Matt dragged his case inside and left it there. He'd have plenty of time to unpack it later. He didn't want to miss their exit from Nyemouth harbour. While Jake untied their mooring ropes, he climbed the ladder to the pilot bridge and took his seat in the passenger chair.

The next eight weeks lay ahead of them. A full trip around the coast of the UK—something Jake had wanted to do for years but hadn't had the opportunity until now. They were about to experience it together.

And down in Matt's suitcase, hidden inside a pair of his socks, was a ring. He didn't know when or where on this voyage he was going to ask Jake to marry him, but he would know the moment when it came. There was no rush, with the open ocean in front of them and all the freedom they wanted.

As Jake edged the boat away from the moorings, the crowd on the dock whooped and cheered.

"Bon voyage."

"Have a great time."

"Enjoy every moment."

Matt and Jake grinned and waved back until they were out of sight.

"Some send-off," Matt said.

"I suspect Lizzie and Jacob cooked it up between them."

Jake stood at the wheel, the wind gently ruffling his hair as he guided the boat towards the river mouth. Matt got up and stood behind him, putting his hands gently on Jake's waist.

"Are you excited?" he asked, his mouth close to Jake's ear and breathing in the fresh smell of him.

"Absolutely buzzing," he said, leaning back against his chest.

The Golden Lady left the shelter of the harbour and sailed into the open sea. Every part of Matt's body tingled.

They were setting out on the adventure of a lifetime.

And he knew, as he held Jake in his arms and breathed in the intoxicating air, it would be the first of many. They had the rest of their lives together.

This was only the beginning.

Want to see more from this author? Here's a taster for you to enjoy!

Success: The Runner
Thom Collins

Excerpt

After a few minutes of light-hearted banter with his co-host Lanita, Alex Shaefer brought his weekly podcast to a close. There were never enough hours in the day for Alex to achieve all the things he wanted, and with today's recording running half an hour over, time was getting tight.

"Nice one," Lanita said, reaching across the desk to give him a high-five.

"Is that everything?" Alex asked their producer Naz. "Have we got enough?"

Naz gave a thumbs-up through the studio window. "All good."

Alex let out a long exhalation and took off his headphones.

The Long Run was Alex's baby. The podcast was coming to the end of a second successful year that had seen it move from being an independent broadcast in its first seven months onto the wider platform of the BBC. The original concept had been to focus on British athletics, but they had widened their remit to cover all aspects of sport. Lanita Khan, a well-known football pundit, had joined the team when the show expanded, taking it to even greater triumphs.

With success came more work. The show took longer than ever to put together—booking guests, researching subjects and covering all the latest sports news and gossip. It was a relentless cycle each week. As a sideline, it had almost become a full-time job in itself. At least the move to the BBC had saved him from having to chase the sponsorship and funding deals that had been essential for them as an indie. Because podcasts were free to listen to and so many kids were doing them for fun from their bedrooms, a lot of people were surprised to learn how expensive it was to put a professional-sounding show together and get it on the air.

It was done—for today, at least. Tomorrow the work would start all over on next week's production.

Alex ran his fingers through his dark brown hair, pushing it back from his forehead in thick waves.

"Relax," Lanita said, obviously noticing his tension.

"I can't help it. You know how much I hate having to do the front and centre promotion. That stuff kills me."

Lanita grinned. "Babe, I don't want to sound rude, but you've got nothing to worry about. Sure, you wrote the book, but no one will pay you much attention. You know that, right? All eyes will be on Fernando."

"I hope that's true," he said, unconvinced.

Tonight was the launch of *Playing with Pride*, the official autobiography of Fernando Inglesias. Fernando had made headlines late in the past year when he'd become the first premiership footballer to come out as gay. It was sensational news, which had caused headlines around the world. Everybody had wanted his story. At the time, Alex had dedicated an entire episode of the podcast to the issue of homophobia, not just in football but in sport in general. It was one of his most streamed shows and had resulted in him being asked to speak on several TV programmes.

It had been a huge shock to receive a call three weeks later, asking if he'd like to write Fernando's story for a book. Alex had ghostwritten three other sporting biographies, and the experience had been far from fulfilling. The majority of the subjects for those biographies were people who had no interest in books or even reading, beyond the advance they were offered from the publishers. Sitting down with a writer to flesh out the details of their life and career was often the last thing any of the sporting icons wanted to do. It had been a dismal experience working with those people.

"Things will be different this time." That was what he'd been promised. He'd have unrestricted access to Fernando for the period of research and full credit for having written the book, not just a mention in the acknowledgement section.

Despite his reservations about writing another sports bio, the offer had been too good for him to refuse, and against all expectations, Fernando had come through and acknowledged Alex as his co-writer on *Playing with Pride*. It was a bold step and one which he was grateful for, even when that meant accompanying Fernando on the publicity circuit.

They'd already given joint interviews to several media outlets. *No big deal.* That was part of Alex's business. After completing an MA in sports journalism in his early twenties and gaining his first job at BBC Radio, he'd been in the profession sixteen years and knew how to handle the press.

However, all the other aspects of promotion were a struggle.

To celebrate the book, there would be a huge party in central Manchester. A year after his ground-breaking announcement, Fernando Inglesias was still big news…huge. The pre-sales on *Playing with Pride* were massive. All eyes would be on him, and as his collaborator, Fernando wanted Alex by his side.

"Why don't you tell him you're uncomfortable with this?" Lanita asked.

"I don't want to hurt his feelings. Besides, I've got my name on the cover rather than a ghostwriting credit, so I owe him," Alex said.

"I'm sure he'd understand."

"The trouble is, I think Fernando is nervous too. You know what a big deal this is. He's still the only openly gay player we have. There are plenty of other gay footballers, but no one has followed his lead and come out after him. The guy needs all the support he can get."

She nodded. "And you'll be perfect at it. You always are. Why do *you* get so nervous? You're a natural at what you do."

"Behind the camera," he said. "Radio, podcasting, writing… There's a reason I haven't gone up for any TV presenting jobs. I hate having a camera pointed at me and being the centre of attention."

Lanita rolled her eyes. "You being so unattractive and all."

Alex gave a shy laugh. It wasn't his looks that bothered him about being on camera. He knew he was photogenic, with his strong bone structure and dark hair. Even if he weren't, he didn't care what people thought of him. He just didn't want the attention or adulation that came from appearing on screen or in print — the letters, the emails and IMs that came in the thousands whenever he appeared on TV. There was always a mix of good and bad comments, and they were an unwanted distraction. Alex didn't need any of that to do his job.

As a journalist or reporter, the best asset anyone could have was the ability to walk around unnoticed.

Something inside him clammed up when he was on camera. He could sit in the podcast studio and talk for hours, but the few times he'd been dragged onto TV shows, he'd found himself unable to articulate or express any of the points he needed to make.

He was in a minority. Plenty of other journalists sought fame and attention from TV and social media, and they were welcome to every bit of it.

Alex didn't need or want it.

Lanita gathered her things together, stuffing them inside a huge red leather bag. "C'mon. Let's go. I'm taking you for a drink."

Alex shook his head. "I can't. I have to go home to get ready for the party."

"Bitch, please. What are you going to do? Take a shower and change your shirt? You can do that in fifteen minutes. I know what you're like when you go out, and you don't need two hours to achieve it. C'mon. We're going—me, you and Naz. You know we can't make this evening, and we want to celebrate the book too. I'm buying, so you'd better take advantage of that while you can."

They recorded the podcast at a studio in Media City close to Salford Quays and an array of trendy bars and restaurants. Ten minutes later, they were settled in a comfortable booth with a bottle of champagne on the table.

"To Alex and Fernando," Lanita said, raising a toast.

They clinked glasses.

"When are we gonna get him on the show?" Naz asked. "Fernando, I mean. If anyone can pull a few strings, it's got to be you. We should be all over this book release."

Naz was a good ten years younger than Alex and Lanita but knew more about broadcast technology and recording than the two of them combined. He was a talented kid and had been with the show since the beginning. Alex had picked well when he'd hired him.

"It doesn't feel right, using privilege like that," Alex said. "Besides, there's also the BBC policy about advertising. I can't plug my own book on the show."

"Bullshit," Naz and Lanita said in unison.

"You don't have to mention the book at all," Naz continued. "We just want an interview with Fernando. You know what he would do for our listening figures. Ask him about it tonight."

"No," Alex said firmly. "I'm not going to exploit our friendship for listeners."

"I would," Lanita said. "If I was going to the launch, I wouldn't hesitate. And he would say yes. I'm sure of it."

"How come you're not going?" Naz asked.

"I'm presenting a feature on *The One Show*. Can't get out of it," she said, taking a sip of champagne. "It's bound to be some party. I heard the pre-sales are the biggest in years for a football book. They expect it to be bigger than Beckham's. Your publisher will have money to burn. There are bound to be some big names around tonight."

"Oh, please don't say that," Alex protested. "I feel nervous enough as it is."

"There's are players and managers going from Liverpool and Manchester," she continued undeterred. "Soap stars, musicians, athletes. Ethan Bower, Rory Evans, Moses Adebayo... They're all going."

Alex froze, backtracking on what she had just said — one name in particular.

"Ethan Bower?" he said. "He's going?"

"Sure. All of them are."

Naz grinned at Alex across the table. "Doesn't he, like, hate you?"

Alex grimaced. "I have no idea."

Naz laughed. "I think you do."

"What's this?" Lanita perked up, a huge smile on her face as she put down her glass. "What have I missed?"

"Nothing," Alex said.

"Alex and Ethan Bower have history," Naz chuckled.

Lanita turned to Alex, her pretty eyes sparkling. "OMG. You haven't shagged him, have you? Tell me you didn't."

"I didn't," he protested. "It's nothing like that."

She groaned. "Pity. Then what? Come on. Spill the story? And how come I don't know this already?"

"It's no big secret," Alex said, shooting Naz a dirty look. "I ghostwrote Ethan's autobiography, which came out about eight years ago."

"You did? I don't even remember him having a book out."

"With good reason. It was a busy time with a lot of big-name biographies vying for the Christmas market. His book kind of got lost in the crowd. It didn't really bother me. As a ghostwriter, they paid me a flat fee. Whether the book was a success or bombed, I got paid just the same."

"So, what's the big deal? Does he think it's your fault his book flopped? I mean, how old was he, anyway? In his twenties? He can't have had much of a story to tell at that age."

Naz cleared his throat theatrically and read aloud from the screen of his phone. "Quote... *'The man who wrote my book didn't do his research and was poorly informed. He seemed like a nice enough guy when we sat down for the interviews, but when he wrote it up, he did a real hatchet job on me. What's written in that book are not my words. He made it up so I would sound like a shallow, egotistical arsehole. I tried to get him fired and hire someone new, but it was too late. The book had to be in the shops by a certain date, and there just wasn't time to start over. I'm glad it didn't do well in the end, so less people got to read that bullshit. Jesus, that guy was a prick.'* End quote." Naz put down the phone, his eyes twinkling with mischief.

"A hatchet job," Lanita said. "Classy."

Alex sighed and swallowed some champagne. It tasted bitter all of a sudden. "That's Ethan's version of what happened."

"And how does your version differ?" she asked. "Dramatically, no doubt."

"The part about him being a shallow, egotistical arsehole... I didn't make that up. It was all there to begin with. All I did was put his personality on the page."

"I've always found him quite charming," she said.

"You know him?"

"A little. Not so much from his competition days, but I've met him recently. In fact, I saw him just last month on a breakfast show, and he was very nice. I wouldn't call him an arsehole at all."

"Maybe he's mellowed. I met him at the height of his success."

Ethan Bower was one of the UK's most triumphant sprinters. He'd won silver and gold medals at both the 2012 and 2016 Olympic Games for the four-hundred-metre races, as well as sharing team glory in the relays. With his wholesome good looks and dazzling green eyes, Ethan had been the poster boy for British athletics when Alex had been approached to pen his biography.

Alex had leapt at the opportunity. Ethan had been one of the UK's most exciting stars…a hero.

Ethan had proved to Alex that the adage of never meeting your heroes was true. With reddish-blond hair, Ethan had the fiery temper to match. As Alex spent time with him for the purpose of the book, he'd witnessed first-hand Ethan's obnoxious behaviour. He'd treated everyone as if they were beneath him — his coach, trainers, physios, ground attendants, reporters and even his fans. He'd been mean-spirited and aggressive and focused on nothing other than his own achievements. His apparent lack of empathy or understanding of others had caused Alex to question more than once whether or not Ethan was a psychopath.

Alex had raised his concerns with the publisher at the time — that he didn't think he could present an impartial view of Ethan, after everything he'd witnessed. They had dismissed his unease. They needed the book in a hurry and didn't care how it was written. Ethan already had a reputation as a bad boy of athletics. No one wanted to read a sanitized version of his story.

"*Throw it all in,*" his editor had advised.

The experience of writing the book had almost put Alex off ghostwriting for life.

Thankfully, none of his other subjects had turned out to be as difficult as Ethan.

"He's pretty hot," Lanita said. "He was always a good-looking guy, but have you seen him recently? OMG, time has been very kind. He's unbelievably fine."

"It doesn't matter what he looks like," Alex said. "It's what's on the inside that counts, and from what I saw, the inside of that man is the worst kind of brat."

"You might be surprised. What you're describing does not sound like the man I know. He was charming, well-spoken…quite humble, in fact."

Alex spluttered, almost choking on his drink. "Humble? Ethan Bower? You have definitely got the wrong guy—not unless he's had a personality transplant. 'Toxic' is the best word I can think of to describe him."

She shrugged. "Well, like I said earlier, it's going to be a big party. You probably won't even see him if he's there. Don't let it spoil your night. It's about you and Fernando, not Ethan."

"Too right," he said. "And if I do see him, you can be sure I'll give him a wide berth. He doesn't like me, and I don't like him. I don't think we have anything to achieve in speaking to each other."

About the Author

Thom Collins is the author of Closer by Morning, with Pride Publishing. His love of page turning thrillers began at an early age when his mother caught him reading the latest Jackie Collins book and promptly confiscated it, sparking a life-long love of raunchy novels.

Thom has lived in the North East of England his whole life. He grew up in Northumberland and now lives in County Durham with his husband and two cats. He loves all kinds of genre fiction, especially bonkbusters, thrillers, romance and horror. He is also a cookery book addict with far too many titles cluttering his shelves. When not writing he can be found in the kitchen trying out new recipes. He's a keen traveler but with a fear of flying that gets worse with age, but since taking his first cruise in 2013 he realized that sailing is the way to go.

Thom loves to hear from readers. You can find his contact information, website details and author profile page at https://www.pride-publishing.com

Sign up for our newsletter and find out about all our romance book releases, eBook sales and promotions, sneak peeks and FREE romance books!